The Gay Detective

The Gay Detective

Lou Rand

CLEIS
PRESS

Published in the United States by Cleis Press Inc.,
P.O. Box 14684, San Francisco, California 94114.
Printed in the United States.
Cover design: Scott Idleman
Text design: Karen Quigg
Cleis Press logo art: Juana Alicia
10 9 8 7 6 5 4 3 2 1

Introduction: Mystery as History

Susan Stryker and Martin Meeker

Lou Rand's *The Gay Detective* is a genre-busting gem of a story written in the waning days of the golden age of American "pulp" paperback publishing. Until now it has been largely forgotten by readers and disparaged by the few critics who ever took notice of it, but we think you'll agree as you peruse the following pages that the book deserves a wider contemporary audience.

The Gay Detective can best be described as "hard-boiled camp." The plot revolves around a grisly murder/blackmail/narcotics racket, but the cast of characters includes a gracefully aging chorus boy who packs a pistol and carries a private investigator's license, a down-on-his luck football stud who might not be as shocked as one might expect upon learning that some boys do more than bathe in a bathhouse, and a vivacious vixen with a taste for rough trade and a roomful of kinky secrets. Along the way we meet handsome thugs, catty drag queens, sleazy businessmen, corrupt cops, tainted politicians, and a gossip columnist who bears more than a passing resemblance to the late, great *San Francisco Chronicle* newspaper columnist Herb Caen.

The Gay Detective is set in "Bay City," a thinly disguised San Francisco. The action takes place in the late 1950s and early 1960s, just as that fabled city was earning its reputation as a world-renowned gay gathering-spot. While this tightly plotted little book offers a fun time for readers who don't know a thing about San Francisco's queer past, to those in the know, *The Gay Detective* also provides a fascinating guide to a place known since the mid-19th century as "Sodom By the Sea." It's a history, as well as a mystery—and it's written by a man almost as mysterious, and just as historically noteworthy, as the characters he created.

San Francisco isn't the only thing about *The Gay Detective* that's thinly disguised. "Lou Rand" supplies only slight cover for chef and writer Lou Rand Hogan, who under the name Lou Hogan penned regular items for *Sunset* and *Gourmet* magazines. The historical record reveals little about the man, but the few anecdotes and pieces of evidence that have survived are all intriguing. He was born in Los Angeles at the turn of the last century and moved to San Francisco as a young man in the 1920s. Those two California cities would remain his principal ports-of-call over the next several decades, but his career as a chef took him to exotic locales around the globe. Hogan worked as a chef aboard the Matson luxury liner *Lurline* on its regular San Francisco to Honolulu to Sydney run, he served in the Royal Canadian Air Force, and ruled the roost in such exclusive Bay Area dining rooms as those of the Bohemian Club, the Palace Hotel, and the Mark Hopkins. At other times he worked as a personal chef for billionaire industrialist Henry J. Kaiser and for the Sultan of Jahore in Singapore.

While dishing up Continental cuisine for the rich and famous, Hogan also took time to dish in print about two central features of his life: food and the gay world. He achieved his widest public with his *Gourmet* and *Sunset* gigs, but later in life he also contributed to *The Advocate*, San Francisco's *Bay Area Reporter*, and other gay publications. Hogan's twin passions intertwined most famously—and notoriously—in *The Gay Cookbook*. This "compendium of campy cuisine," published in 1965 by Sherbourne Press in Los Angeles, gained a cult following and went through numerous printings. The cookbook's readers were treated to serious haute cuisine recipes as well as generous servings of vintage '60s humor— an unrelenting cascade of double entendre that played on the apparently endless parallels between the kitchen and the bedroom. Hogan's introduction for "Browned Beef Stew" clearly demands a parenthetical reference to "browning" and "frenching." The book's decidedly male (and often overtly misogynistic) bias is made clear by the disclaimer that it contains no recipes for fish.

Hogan's adventurous life ended with little fanfare in Los Angeles in 1976. He left no known heirs, no will, no correspondence or personal papers. Apart from his essays and books, the man left few traces of his private life. Based on a brief, unpublished essay written by Hogan, we know that he considered the pseudonymous Robert Scully's early gay novel *The Scarlet Pansy* (1932), which chronicled the party-filled life of a beautiful boy named Fay in the years around World War I, to be the most accurate representation of the kind of life Hogan himself had led. Moreover, Hogan wrote that *The Scarlet Pansy* was a "noteworthy book" because "it marked the beginning of a world-wide social trend"—gay literature. He admired the book so much that he hoped his short essay would be the introduction to a reissue of the work, but these plans never came to fruition.

Most of what we do know about Hogan is derived from a short series of reminiscences he published as "The Golden Age of Queens" in 1974 in the *Bay Area Reporter,* under the nom de plume Toto Le Grand. Hogan's persistent use of pseudonyms might appear odd to out-and-proud gay readers today, but he acted as did most gay men of his generation, prizing privacy and anonymity over the double-edged sword of notoriety. Those reminiscences offer intriguing insights into the real-life underpinnings of *The Gay Detective*, written against a backdrop of sweeping historical change in the city of San Francisco, in the organization of "old gay life," and in the relationships between sexuality, vice, and crime at a time when homosexuality was itself illegal. In them, we see much of Hogan's character and personal style, and are treated to a few juicy anecdotes that paint a telling picture of the society in which he moved. Hogan made it clear that during the Roaring Twenties the most raucous gay life appeared on the street. "Looking back," he wrote, "it must be repeated that Market Street was the focal point of all the action; remember, up until 1932, there were no bars open as such, you 'met' on the street. Every foot of it, from the Anchor Bar at the Embarcadero corner to the Crystal Palace Market, could tell a story, all interesting." Along with engaging in the "promenade" up and down the street "to show off new 'outfits', hair-do's, jewels, and the like," Hogan wrote about one of the "interesting" stories that unfolded in the Unique Theater, formerly located on Market Street between Third and Fourth. Originally opened as a grand movie palace during the Silent Era, by the late 1920s "this old grind house," according to Hogan, had fallen into disrepair and it was a place one might find a "middle-of-the-night trick." Hogan added that because "the house was kept so dark (to hide its grime) one could DO the trick right in his seat, if one were agile enough. This was quite often managed!"

The celebratory, sex-affirming tone so evident in "The Golden Age of the Queens" did not secure a lasting literary reputation for Lou Rand Hogan. He has gone entirely unmentioned in queer-focused encyclopedias, "who's who" lists, and other reference works. *The Gay Detective* similarly has been overlooked in the numerous anthologies of gay literature and historical overviews of gay fiction that have now been produced. *The Gay Detective* was initially published in 1961 by Saber Press of Fresno, California, and the history of that publishing house helps explain some of the obscurity that has surrounded *The Gay Detective* since its initial appearance. Saber Press was owned and operated by Sanford Aday, allegedly a former pimp, and his partner Wallace de Ortega Maxey, an ordained minister and early member of the pioneering gay rights group the Mattachine Society. Most Saber Press books—with titles like *I Peddle Jazz, Camera Bait,* and *Our Flesh Was Cheap*—dealt with lurid, semi-sleazy topics. They had low production values and limited distribution, but they were quite tame compared to the graphic pornography that would begin to appear before the end of the 1960s. Saber's proprietors repeatedly ran afoul of the law in that more censorious era; after selling a copy of *Sex Life of a Cop* through their mail order business to a customer in Grand Rapids, Michigan, Aday and Maxey were convicted of shipping lewd materials through the mails. They were fined $10,000 and sentenced to several years in prison.

Although lesbian works of various quality and veracity abounded (and sold well) in the "golden age" of paperback publishing between World War II and the rise of the sexual liberation movement in the mid-1960s, print representations of gay male life were harder to come by and faced greater barriers to distribution. In a culture where straight men might take voyeuristic pleasure in fantasizing about lesbian sexual scenes (and thus provide a wide non-lesbian audience for lesbian-themed paperbacks), books with gay male themes were targeted primarily at a gay male audience, and were much more vulnerable to homophobic legal attacks. Consequently, even paperback works that had some substance, like *The Gay Detective*, were relegated to publishing houses that survived in the margins of respectability. To a certain extent, the taint of disreputability has always clung to Hogan's novel, both in its initial release by Saber and its subsequent republication under the title *Rough Trade* (with a slightly revised text), by Argyle Books in 1964.

When post-gay-liberation literary scholars have taken note of *The Gay Detective* at all, one senses a trace of embarrassment in their dismissive tone. Roger Austen, in his seminal 1977 book, *Playing the Game: The Homosexual Novel in America*, says that Hogan's novel was nothing more than "tepid." James Levine's 1991 survey, *The Homosexual Novel in America*, takes an even more critical tack. Levine writes, "Lou Rand's *Gay Detective* is an inferior mystery novel with some feeble attempt at humor.... Throughout most of the novel, gays emerge as stereotypically effeminate queens. The story of a gay detective who solves the crimes committed by those preying on gay men sounds positive, but this is not the case. The few masculine gay men are the murder victims. The police chief, who is aware of the crime syndicate, and his friend who ran it both escape prosecution.... In short, the blackmailing of gay men is shown as only mildly reprehensible and popular stereotypes of gay men were not disputed."

Levine's concern with effeminate stereotypes lies at the heart of Hogan's negligible critical reputation. Hogan himself identified as an effeminate "queen," and he wrote his book in the then contemporary "queen's vernacular" of a now-vanished gay male world. Hogan's milieu was organized along butch/queen lines that resembled in some respects the better-known butch/femme gender system of the lesbian world. He was consequently neglected by a generation (or two) of gay editors whose political sensibilities were forged in reaction to that older gay way of life, and who were more comfortable with newer styles of gay masculinity that disparaged effeminacy.

In fairness to Hogan's critics, charges of effeminacy have been historically important ways of oppressing gay men; it is equally true that some critiques of effeminacy harbor a masculinist bias against the feminine. We as contemporary readers have an opportunity to step outside the ideologically motivated frameworks of previous decades, however, to reappraise older literary works in their historical context—indeed, the glimpses we catch of social realities that no longer exist provide much of the pleasure of such texts. *The Gay Detective* is admittedly light fare, perhaps tepid in its lack of sexual explicitness and stereotypical in its representations of gay male gender conventions, but to dismiss the book's worthiness on those grounds reveals more about the assumptions and agendas of contemporary critics than they do about the ultimate value of Hogan's detective story.

And in the end—whatever one thinks about the dated language, corny humor, unfortunate anglocentric prejudices, or politically incorrect representations of gender and sexuality—Hogan's novel is primarily a detective story. On this level the book succeeds wonderfully, and readers will just have to find out for themselves whodunit and why. Rather than spoiling the plot, however, we want to act as tour guides to the San Francisco on which Hogan patterned his fictional Bay City, alerting readers to the local color and sites of historical interest they'll encounter when following the main characters on Hogan's fabulously fruity tour of a seedy sexual underground.

Mystery writing and historical studies might seem at first glance to be worlds apart: mysteries are generally fiction and histories are ostensibly fact; mystery authors write to delight and confound the reader while historians write to educate and explain; mystery novels generally end with all loose threads being tied up, while histories generally wind up posing more questions than they can answer. There are similarities, too, of course. Investigation, hypothesis, and evidence are important features of both genres, as the writer constructs a narrative designed to gradually reveal some version of truth. And as is often the case in sleuthing of either sort, some of the most revealing evidence is found not through conscious acts of seeking, but rather in stumbling upon something unexpected.

This is precisely how *The Gay Detective* came to our attention. While working on their 1996 book *Gay by the Bay*, a history of queer culture in the San Francisco Bay Area, Susan Stryker and her co-author Jim Van Buskirk skimmed through the San Francisco Public Library's vast, recently-acquired collection of lesbian and gay paperbacks, assembled by lesbian publisher Barbara Grier of Naiad Press, looking for San Francisco–related materials. *The Gay Detective* was one such find. Neither Stryker nor Van Buskirk spent much time at that point digging into the novel's historical background, and contented themselves with reproducing the cover art for a pictorial spread in *Gay by the Bay*.

A few years later Stryker shared the book with the San Francisco Queer History Working Group, whose other members included Martin Meeker, Willie Walker, Gayle Rubin, and Paul Gabriel. That's when the historically grounded nature of the novel's back story became visible, as nearly half a dozen historians pieced together what they knew about various aspects of San Francisco's mid-century history based on their own original research. The group members quickly realized that while Hogan's detective tale offered an enjoyable evening's read, it also supplied something far more substantial: a veritable road-map to the inner dynamics of "pre-liberation" gay culture. That realization is what prompted us to seek republication of this neglected and forgotten work, with a new historical introduction.

Even in its most superficial details, *The Gay Detective* is so chock full of references to the contemporary culture of San Francisco that the book practically begs for historical analysis. The Backroom Crowd at Flanagan's Bar, to whom we are introduced in the second chapter and whose centrality to the plot is revealed only towards the end of the book, are all modeled on prominent San Francisco figures. Jake Eberhart is based on headline-conscious society lawyer Jake Ehrlich, who had gained a name for himself defending the likes of Billie Holiday and notorious madam Sally Stanford—and for having his victories published in the book *Never Plead Guilty*. Senator Martin resembles real-life Senator (and former San Francisco Mayor) James K. Phelan who, like his fictional counterpart, was a "confirmed bachelor" hailing from the highest rungs of the social ladder. Joe Cannelli, a night club operator with a "live and let live" attitude towards the city's burgeoning homosexual population, has more in common with Joe Finocchio—proprietor of the famous female impersonator venue Finocchio's—than an Italian surname. Then there's gossip-columnist Bert Kane, a fine caricature of three-dot journalist Herb Caen. In spite of his apparently vigorous heterosexuality, Caen's generally good-natured columns displayed on occasion such intimate knowledge of his beloved city's gay life that rumors persisted about his own sexual practices. As Hogan says of Caen's fictional alter ego in *The Gay Detective*, "anyone knowing that much of the words and music is bound to have done the dance routines too."

Like the supporting cast of characters, many of the story's locales are drawn from the material world. Canneli's *Bait Room* is not quite Finocchio's, but it's a reasonable facsimile of "Fin's" chief competitor, the slightly more down-market and risqué Beige Room, which was located on Broadway at the crossroads of North Beach, Chinatown, and Nob Hill. Likewise, the generically named Baths bathhouse, where the novel's climactic action takes place, also had a brick and mortar prototype, Dave's Baths, situated near the waterfront on the edge of North Beach. Hogan goes so far as to mention the controversial new Embarcadero Freeway (whose construction would soon be halted by the grass-roots "freeway revolt") then being built adjacent to Dave's. One of the book's cleverest settings—a gym by day, an illicit after-hours club by night—actually existed in San Francisco's then mostly black Fillmore neighborhood, but Hogan, the cheeky chef, fictionalized the Gourmet Club as the Gourmand Club.

More significant than the myriad parallels between characters and places are the situations that motivate the plot. Blackmail is at the heart of the story, and in this respect, too, Hogan draws on lived experience. The fear of exposure as a homosexual that led Hogan to mask his identity in much of his explicitly gay writing has been a persistent feature of gay life, one that was even more prevalent in earlier decades of the 20th century than it has been recently. In his autobiographical "The Golden Age of the Queens," Hogan makes the shocking admission that he himself had stooped to blackmail in the dark days of the Great Depression—befriending straight military officers at tony Nob Hill hotel bars, stealing their wallets to learn their identities and addresses, and later demanding money in exchange for not spilling the beans to the men's wives and commanders. Usually, however, the exploitation worked in the other direction, with countless gay and bisexual men ruining themselves financially to avoid the social stigma of public accusations of homosexuality.

Interestingly, given the historical veracity of much else in Hogan's novel, there are tantalizing clues in another mid-century gay paperback about a blackmail ring in San Francisco. Bud Clifton's otherwise forgettable *Muscle Boy* (Ace, 1958), also set in the Bay Area, details a scam quite similar in its particulars to the one uncovered by Hogan's gay detective. In describing *Muscle Boy* in his 1964-65 Guild Book Service mail order catalog of gay-interest titles, pioneering anti-censorship activist H. Lynn Womack notes that "this thinly disguised fiction" allows readers familiar with the San Francisco scene to "enjoy identifying" the characters, "because they are from real life, as real as life around... California can be."

Less apparent to the casual reader is the way in which the spatial organization of semi-public and commercial sexual activity in Hogan's Bay City mimics what local historians have uncovered about the interrelationships between mid-century San Francisco's gay neighborhoods and commercial sex and "vice" districts. Without giving away too many details of the plot, gay detective Francis Morley and his sidekick Tiger Olsen follow a trail of crime that begins in a high-profile night-spot patronized by "slumming" socialites, tourists, and open-minded "bohemians" as well as by gay men and lesbians. The action then moves to a more marginal after-hours joint before finally arriving at the steamy, seamy Baths.

In the process, the protagonists move from a tourist-oriented entertainment district, to an inner-city slum, to a derelict waterfront, all the while moving deeper and deeper into a criminalized underworld of illegal drugs and sexual variance. In doing so they map a circuit through which the city's sexual appetites once circulated. What seems most fascinating here is the way in which Hogan's story depends on the consequences of criminalizing all sorts of non-reproductive erotic activity and pleasure-seeking stimulation, as well as on the unexpected couplings of high society with low life that transpire in the shadowy back-ways of the city. Buried beneath all the fluff, Hogan's book offers a serious political critique: he shows how social privilege is preserved by casting non-normative sexuality out into the margins of society, but also how the sexual margins are preserved precisely because they offer a space for the socially privileged to enact desires and practices condemned by an oppressive and hypocritical society. It was in this space, structured by the needs of elites, that pre-liberation gay life was allowed to flourish, and to be exploited.

Exploitation is the hinge upon which the sexual double standard turned. In true *noir* style, Hogan depicts a world whose very order depends upon outlaw spaces over which cops and criminals—two rival gangs—vie for the ability to profit from the people and activities relegated to the sexual margins. Even more impressively, however, the back story Hogan offers as motivating force for his foregrounded tale of blackmail and murder involves a sense of sweeping historical change. He shows how broad social developments that had nothing directly to do with homosexuality nevertheless worked to disrupt and reconfigure the underworld of vice and crime in ways that led to the emergence of new—and newly politicized—gay identities and communities.

In a pivotal scene in which gay private detective Francis Morley is called in to help the Bay City Police Department solve a string of murders involving gay men, we learn that the law has taken an interest in the murders primarily because there seems to be some connection between the murders and a new movement of narcotics into the city. An FBI agent assigned to the case, clearly uncomfortable with the gay angle that has emerged in the investigation, asks the local police officers why Bay City "has such an overlarge percentage of these queer people." In response, Captain Morphy, head of the Bay City Vice Squad (who may be modeled on a notorious Sergeant Frank Murphy, much reviled by the gay community of San Francisco for his zeal in targeting homosexuals for arrest) offers a lengthy explanation that reveals much of Hogan's historical vision:

> Y'see, this town used to be wide open. It was the talk of the world, being a seaport and all. Things were pretty much under control, and everyone was making a little money. Then these people that always want to clean up everything—well, it seems that after they lost out on prohibition, they decided to run all the 'hoors' out of town. Finally, we had to close up all those quiet, friendly, well-regulated houses.... This put all the girls on the streets and hustling in bars, unregulated and uninspected, too. Even this didn't satisfy the 'do-gooders.' First we had to run 'em off the streets, and now it's outa the bars, too. I dunno. This is a sailor's town. It was once a great port. I guess these young fellas today just gotta do something with the time on their hands.

Hogan's implication that male homosexuality increased in San Francisco between the end of Prohibition and the early

1960s because of a lack of female prostitutes needs to be taken with a grain of salt, but his story of shifting relations between the police department and the sex industry is an accurate account of what happened in San Francisco in the 1930s, '40s, and '50s. With the closure of the old Barbary Coast through the Red-Light Abatement Act in 1917, most prostitution in the city became concentrated in the downtown "Tenderloin," which was under the tight control of the corrupt, bribe-and-kickback taking cops of the Central Station. Prostitution had been allowed to flourish in the Tenderloin since the 19th century, as long as the police got their share of the financial action. Street-walking was not allowed; the police would steer sex workers they encountered to one of the many houses of prostitution that offered police pay-offs in exchange for the privilege of doing business without interference. At one point in the early 20th century, the city of San Francisco had even tried to legalize prostitution, as long as sex workers remained in the Tenderloin and visited a municipal health clinic twice a week to test for sexually transmitted disease. The police force would have none of it, because legalization undermined their lucrative extortion racket, and they successfully brought pressure to bear on elected officials through a cynically manipulated morality crusade to have prostitution recriminalized. By the late 1950s and early 1960s, however, powerful constituencies whose ideas of civic virtue differed from those of a corrupt Central Station police force had begun to break down the well-established, self-interested "regulation" of inner-city prostitution.

Contesting police control of the Tenderloin "vice trade" was related to changes in the physical fabric of San Francisco and the wider Bay Area. In the years after World War II, which saw a dramatic increase in the region's population, a sweeping regional master plan was put in place that, over the ensuing quarter century, gradually transformed San Francisco's downtown into a financial nexus for the Pacific Rim, moved much of the city's heavy industry and port facilities across the bay to Oakland, encouraged a large-scale migration to the suburbs through cheap home loans, and interconnected the entire region with a new system of freeways and mass transit (BART—the Bay Area Rapid Transit system). The social and economic dislocations wrought by these spatial changes—like the withering away of San Francisco's maritime trade mentioned by Captain Morphy—dramatically changed the "sexual ecology" of inner-city San Francisco. The police struggled to retain a grip on their traditional turf, but they were swimming against the tide of the times.

Hogan connects the emergence of a newly visible gay community at this moment in time with the broader social shifts he noted. When the federal agent asks Morphy what his discourse on prostitution has to do with "all these open 'fag' bars and joints," Morphy replies:

> Personally, I always want to plant a foot in those cuties' butts, but the new Commission has psychiatrists now who advise that these people should be allowed to congregate in their own places. I suppose it does eliminate a lot of friction—fights and stuff that might get started in regular joints. Yeah, and it does make it easier for us in a sense, 'cause we can keep an eye on them better.

A visible gay community, Hogan implies, resulted in part from the loss of traditional opportunities for corrupt police vice regulation. Significantly, at the very time Hogan was writing, San Francisco newspapers carried stories of the so-called "Gayola" scandal, in which owners of gay bars, emboldened by a recent California Supreme Court decision protecting the rights of homosexuals to congregate in public places, blew the whistle on several beat cops who had been demanding payoffs for protection from police raids.

Another thread of Morphy's account involves the introduction of narcotics into San Francisco in the 1950s—which, as the plot of *The Gay Detective* subsequently reveals, implicates nightclub owner Joe Cannelli and suggests his connections with Italian crime syndicates. This, too, has its correlates in San Francisco's mid-century history. In an interview with historian Paul Gabriel on file at the GLBT Historical Society, former San Francisco Police Chief Tom Cahill describes how the Italian Mafia tried moving into San Francisco in 1948, with limited success. High-ranking police officers kept the airport under constant surveillance, and would meet suspected Mafiosi at the gate as they deplaned. In the days before the Miranda ruling, a great deal of information could be extracted from suspicious characters without paying as much attention to due process as we have become accustomed to in the past few decades. In Cahill's words, there was a minor Mafia presence in San Francisco, but it "never got off the ground."

Other oral history work does suggest that an Italian-connected narcotics ring operated out of Finocchio's night club in the 1950s, though perhaps without the direct knowledge or involvement of owner Joe Finocchio, who was never personally implicated in any of the surviving accounts. One former performer there recalled how the club was always filled with men in "neon-lit suits" who did a brisk trade in drugs, and how a boyfriend she met there claimed to be involved in a drug-smuggling operation involving military personnel at the Presidio. Although no hard documentary evidence of Mafia-connected narcotics schemes in San Francisco's mid-20th century gay subculture has come to our attention, there are at the very least suggestions in the historical record that the organized criminal activity Hogan describes in *The Gay Detective* had some basis in reality—or at least in the folklore of San Francisco's queer community.

It seems significant to note as well that the struggle between cops and criminals portrayed in Hogan's book carries overtones of ethnic rivalry—the crooks are Italian, while the crooked cops are Irish. Irish-Americans had in fact controlled the San Francisco police force and the vice trades associated with police corruption for decades, compelling members of other ethnic communities looking for a piece of the action to adopt a more entrepreneurial approach. Reading between the lines of Hogan's suggestive comments, Irish cops (in his fictional Bay City, at least) regarded the gay life as part of the profitable underworld of regulated vice that was even then slipping away from them, while criminals associated with dope-pushing Italian mobsters tolerated—and to an extent catered to—homosexuals as an eminently exploitable class of people.

One of the most interesting elements of this power struggle, however, is that its battles are fought in a language that is neither Irish nor Italian, so to speak—but rather, the queen's vernacular. This is precisely the point at which

Francis Morley, the gay detective, appears on the scene. And while it is certainly true that Morley embodies the stereotype of the effeminate gay queen, at a telling moment in his dialog with the police and the FBI, Morley suggests that the persona of "queen" is a mask that he can drop at will:

"Gentlemen, let's face it. Suppose we put it this way, and stop mincing words."

Strangely, and surprisingly to his listeners, his words were now clipped and sincere, and his tone distinguished by a dangerously steely quality that they had not heard from him before.

"Our immediate target seems to be a gang, or organization, that blackmails and dopes the 'boys.'"

Turning to the government agent, Francis continued, "I understand from what you said before that you tried to work your way into a few places, but just didn't seem to fit. The point here seems to be that I look to be more the type, and can probably crash this outfit somewhere."

It's not too much to suggest that in this single scene in a critically dismissed book of lightweight genre fiction, published on the fly and promptly forgotten more than forty years ago, we can see the early glimmer of a new gay sensibility. In the briefest of moments, by artfully switching from queen to butch through the slightest adjustment of his vocal style, Morley reveals to those in power that their assumptions and perceptions of gay life have blinded them to one of the biggest developments in 20th century American urban culture—the emergence of a massive, politically savvy homosexual community. In the moment that Morley announces his intention to help 'the boys' we see that he is not interested merely in a few gangland murders, but rather in working to secure a safe haven for thousands of former chorus boys like himself who would call someplace like Bay City home.

That moment alone is worth the cover price of this Cleis Press reissue of *The Gay Detective*, but we trust you'll enjoy the rest of the book, too, as you cruise the streets of San Fran...—er, we mean Bay City—with the fiercest, feyest private dick ever to sashay out of the Baths in the wee, dark hours of the early morn.

The Gay Detective

Chapter One

The fog-swept park stretched for blocks and blocks, westward through the heart of the city and on to the cold, tide-washed, rocky shore of the ocean. The ever-present damp mist gave an eerie opalescence to the occasional streaks of moonlight that filtered through. The serene quietness of pre-daybreak was broken only by the dim throats of timeless foghorns. Behind the beach and all about the park, Bay City slept—or almost all of it.

From out of those places still awake came a car, a fast sedan. Crazily the big, black car pulled off the highway from the park and shuddered to a jerking halt as it lost traction in the sand. The front doors opened on either side and two men got out. The driver laughed loudly, though slightly off key. He was the younger, well dressed in good but casual sports clothes. Of average height and weight, he carried himself with a noticeably peculiar hauteur, and walked with a short mincing step—almost like a dancer or a model. As he moved around the front of the sedan, his bigger and burlier companion snapped at him in a brusque tone.

"Goddamn it, Kay, turn off the lights!"

This man was young too, though older than the other. He was also handsome, in a brutish, appealing sort of way. His attire was also casual, but his manner was nervous.

Across his heavy forehead, above beetling, coarse brows, was a fine crop of perspiration. His strong muscular hands clinched and unfolded aimlessly. The driver did not seem to notice this tension. He switched off the car's lights and joined his companion. His voice, suited to his figure, was peculiarly light and lilting for a man. It came with a giggle: "Well, Buster, want another crack at him? Or would you go for something a little more lively?"

Almost fiercely the bigger man turned on the other. "Shut up, Kay! Let's get this done with..."

Turning to the rear of the automobile, the big man opened the door and reached into the back of the car. A moment later he heaved a body out onto the sand.

The head of this inert figure was wrapped with a soiled towel; the body was dressed in a dark suit and black shoes. Both men stood hesitantly over the muffled corpse. After a moment's silence, the smaller remarked rather plaintively, "My, why isn't there lots more blood?"

Almost savagely the other replied, "The hell with that! Take his feet. We'll get it down to the water."

The smaller of the two stiffened and shuddered, and struck a disdainful pose. His lower lip trembled, and his hands flustered from limp wrists.

"But, Buster—" he began.

"But Hell! You silly bitch, this is murder. We gotta get it down to the water without leaving any tracks, like if we dragged him. If I carried him I'd get all blood—well, messed up. So we both gotta do it. Now, goddamn you, Kay, pick up his feet."

With this, Buster picked up the shoulders of the body and Kay reluctantly lifted the feet. Down to the water's edge, they trudged crab-wise with their bulky burden, which they dropped at the break of the surf.

A spent wave came in and washed tiredly up the sloping sand. Kay danced nimbly out of its path. Buster reached down and removed the towel from the head of the corpse. The bloodied, battered features stared up sightlessly, and a few locks of abundant hair flowed gently back with the receding waters. The heavy man turned and strode up the beach to the waiting car, the other swiftly behind him, as if afraid to be left alone with that which they had just discarded. Only once did Kay pause. Turning, and with a backward flip of his expressive wrist, he said in a voice that was gaily affected, but quavering, "Well! She'll get her bath tonight, hey, Buster?"

As the two reached the car, Buster stopped to turn and glare speculatively at the other. Kay, now seemingly in a different mood, paused beside the bigger man. With his head thrown back, his throat arched coquettishly, and his eyelids fluttering, Kay seemed almost feminine. Putting his hand gently and caressingly on his companion's muscular arm, he said, petulantly, "You promised, Buster, if I'd help."

After a moment's hesitation, the big man replied roughly, "Okay. Why not? But let's be quick."

Both men climbed into the spacious rear of the sedan and closed the door. A quarter of an hour later they again got out of the car, resumed their original places in the front, and drove swiftly away.

After many blocks the black sedan again stopped, briefly. The burly man got out and strode over to a convenient sewer drain. He stuffed the very soiled towel down into the drain. Returning to the car, he got in and they quickly sped away once more. Quickly and quietly, the two drove into the city that was just awakening.

Chapter Two

Flanagan's, a small bar near Bay City's Hall of Justice, would look to the stranger to be just another small bar. With one or two casual customers and a bored, toothpick-munching bartender, there appeared to be little real justification for the place to be open for business.

Captain of Detectives John Starr, striding into the place, nodded only briefly to the man behind the counter, who never paused in the absorption of his toothpick. Also without pause, Captain Starr strode the length of the premises and passed through a door at the rear.

The room the detective entered was another milieu entirely. Graciously spacious and fitted out as the lounge of an exclusive gentleman's club, this was the famous "Back Room." With several obscure entrances and exits, and with a small service bar as well as a tiny kitchen presided over by an aged and efficient Chinese, the Back Room had been for almost a century the quiet gathering place of many of Bay City's finest citizens. These included judges, lawyers, professional men, a few select businessmen, one or two journalists, and, on occasion over the years, one or two gentlemen connected with the local police.

The "Back Room crowd" was never a membered group, nor were there such devices as dues and meetings. Those who were welcomed came and went as they chose. Others found entrance doors locked, or were simply and quietly turned away by the ageless waiter and bartender, Mr. Grimes, who was the sole arbiter. It was, nevertheless, a quiet and companionable place. By several unwritten but understood rules, pending cases of judges, lawyers, police, and the business of others who might be present, were not discussed. Such news personnel as were admitted seldom quoted anything said or overheard here, and then only with express permission.

As Captain Starr entered he was pleasantly greeted by those who sat about the huge central table. This great round board had often caused the place to be referred to as the "Little Algonquin." Today it was only fairly attended, but by gentlemen all of whom were certainly local personages in their own right.

Next to the detective officer, as he seated himself, was Jay Eberhard, one of the city's leading attorneys, who was frequently referred to as the "Old Master." A quiet appearing and genteel man, one would hardly suspect the number of murderers, embezzlers and other criminals whom he had, temporarily at least, freed from the toils of the law. On the Captain's other hand, and also sitting very quietly and at his ease, holding an ignored drink in his hand, was another figure often seen and read about in the local papers— Senator Martin.

Bruce Martin was a distinguished and cultured gentleman. He had served, very briefly, the remaining part of the term of a deceased state senator. He had likewise taken the bench for a short period upon the demise of a municipal judge. Member, and often chairman, of many private and public committees and bodies, he was surely one of Bay City's most prominent citizens. The Senator was a bachelor. He was past fifty, and was considered to be a man of means. It was also considered that his means had been inherited. At least he had no immediately obvious source of income. Personally, the Senator was a quiet, even-tempered but reticent old gentleman. He always appeared in the most select civic and social groups. Never a fop, he was definitely a man about town.

Though Captain Starr sat down next to the Senator, the latter seemed hardly to notice his presence, aside from a perfunctory greeting. He was seemingly engrossed in conversation with a rather brash appearing young man, Bert Kane, a columnist of Bay City's leading newspaper.

Kane did not write featured stories or national news. Rather in the McIntyre tradition and manner, he sounded off daily about local personages, their fads and foibles. Though young, Kane was clever, and his widely read column was often delightfully humorous and interesting. He was certainly a popular and an obviously discreet newspaperman. His items were personal but never vicious, as currently seemed to be the fashion with certain braying and crusading columnists in eastern cities. Significant in a sense was his welcomed presence in the Back Room. It was to him that Starr addressed himself, after ordering from Mr. Grimes, the ubiquitous waiter.

"Bert, what's the latest that the police should know about but probably don't?" he asked with a smile.

Kane had paused in what he had been saying to the Senator, but before he could reply, a heavy laughing voice from across the table cut in on the interchange. The booming voice of Tiger Olsen, an ex-professional football player, now a used car salesman, cut in with: "Kane's been giving us the lowdown on this guy, or woman, or whatever it is, who went to Denmark and had his marbles removed." Olsen's jolly laughter was infectious and brought out smiles all around the table.

Without letting him finish, the columnist chimed in, "Yeah, but get this for a laugh: At the Council meeting yesterday, the Commissioner started to discuss the suggestion that the city again operate ferries on the Bay. Well, some one loudly remarked that he would like to see more ferries on the Bay and fewer on the streets."

The gentlemen were all amused at this story, though the football player evinced a slight disgust at the type of person indicated.

Tiger Olsen was the youngest of the Back Room group, and had been accepted for the past several years for rather unique reasons. The gentlemen had seldom included an athlete among the older and more professional members. But circumstances had been a bit different with Olsen, who was very popular in many parts of the city. A local boy, in his late teens he had become an outstanding football player and all-around athlete. Snatched up by a nearby university that could afford the best, he had justified their investment by becoming all-American and leading the school's team to many heady victories. While many people would have doubted it, Tiger Olsen had never slighted his studies. He had, in fact, received his sheepskin with very creditable honors. However, almost simultaneously with the diploma, he'd also received an induction notice from Uncle Sam. This he neatly sidestepped by enlisting in the Marine Corps.

On his return to civilian life a few years later as Captain Olsen, and after a very spectacular service career, he was at once feted everywhere as Bay City's most representative hero. Two or three seasons of professional football gave him enough of the game. This was followed by a series of positions and jobs, none of which ever seemed to come to much of anything. At present he represented a firm selling foreign cars.

Behind Olsen's brash and rough surface manner was a good mind and a really pleasant, though actually shy, personality. Of late he had begun to worry about the future. Getting on towards thirty, he had a comfortable nest egg stashed away in the bank. He had hundreds of friends and acquaintances. It was known that a long series of women had enjoyed his company for varying lengths of time and with varying degrees of intimacy.

A psychiatrist would have sensed the inherent shyness of Tiger Olsen. He might have discovered that a good deal of this could have resulted from the name given him by his now deceased parents. The product of a tough neighborhood, he had successfully defended then discarded and lived down the name of Clarence. Very few persons knew the Tiger's real name, and he very pointedly did not offer it. All in all, ran the general opinion, Tiger Olsen was quite a guy.

Another of the group, Joe Cannelli, a rather gross, middle-aged man who ostensibly operated a bar and restaurant, but who was considered by many to be one of the city's leading gamblers, shrugged expressively, and with fair accuracy summed up the local opinion of sexually confused persons: "'Live and let live,' I always say."

Kane laughingly put in: "You always say. But my little

birdie tells me you've got a new bartender at your joint who's very gay."

The restaurateur pretended to be annoyed as he growled, "What the hell. The union sent him. Besides, he's pretty."

Here Captain Starr broke in. "Let me tell you a real funny story, and it happened only this morning. Do any of you remember the old Morley Agency? Old man Morley was one of the first in the city to have a private license."

The attorney nodded. "I remember. He did some jobs for me once or twice. Very reliable. And a very decent old fellow."

Kane interrupted, "Say, didn't he die just last year?"

"That's the fellow," continued the plainclothesman. "Now it seems that he had some steady accounts, quite a sizeable business: skip-tracing, and stuff like that. The lawyers who handled his estate have kept the office open. Some old girl—Morley's secretary for thirty years—has been running it, with some extra help now and then. Well, as I get the story, there was only one heir to whatever was left. They finally located him back East, and now he's out here and is going to take over."

"He in the business too?" queried Olsen. This brought a short laugh from the police officer. "Well, it all depends on what business you mean. He has 'been in the theater,' as he puts it, but it seems to me that he was actually a chorus man in a musical show."

This brought further grins and laughter around the table.

"They say that some of those guys are all man," volunteered the gruff cafe man.

"Not this one," put in Starr. "He came in to get a license and a gun permit. A very pretty fellow with a roving eye. Of course, I could be wrong, but I think…"

"Don't tell us that he made a pass at you, Captain," wryly put in the poker-faced Senator, while more or less obviously looking over the officer's very regular and very masculine features. This, and the Senator's droll manner, brought more hilarious laughter from the group.

"How about it, Starr? Is it, or isn't it?" asked Olsen.

Pausing speculatively before answering, the Captain said, "Hell, you can't always tell these days. But when I asked this character what he needed a gun for, he just rolled his eyes, put his hand on his hip, tossed back his wavy hair and shrieked at me that he'd have a helluva time beating off some attacker with a mascara brush..."

Chapter Three

Hattie Campbell—gray, angular, and efficiently smart—always arrived at the office early. Today in particular she felt that she must be on hand. The new owner, Mr. Francis Morley, was to take over actual charge. While the efficient Miss Campbell had been assured that she would have a place as long as there was an agency, she had an intuitive idea that her private preserve of many orderly years was about to be disrupted.

This new man, old Harry's nephew, had been in and out several times; but the opportunity she had sought for a good, long, get-acquainted talk had just not materialized. Hattie hadn't quite made up her mind whether she liked the young man anyway. After many years as a employee, and later office manager, of a detective agency, she was well aware of the "facts of life." And in Bay City, home of the Arts, culture, bohemianism, and all of the several things that were meant by this last term—things mentioned only in joking—she knew only too well that the simple old classification of "men and women" simply didn't cover the situation any longer.

About Francis Morley, she was puzzled. The guy had charm, manners, and a certain bubbling exuberance, but he was certainly not the man that Harry Morley had been.

And who should know better than Hattie? For thirty years she had been secretary, assistant, mother, companion—everything, in fact, that she could be to Francis Morley's uncle.

There had never been any question of romance for them, but a healthy respect and need for each other instead. The idea of marriage had really never entered their minds. Hattie, at nearly sixty, had been hard hit at Harry's passing, but at his request had kept the old agency going. She had finally located the nephew. Now, she supposed, she could retire. Harry had left her secure. But she felt strongly that she should stick around for a while and help Francis get started.

These last few days she wasn't so sure; this nephew was definitely a character. Sort of on the swish side too, she thought. But maybe that was only the "theater" that had rubbed off on him. She hoped so, anyway, because he really did seem to be a nice person, if just a little too pretty for her tastes.

Well, Hattie mused to herself while going up in the elevator, the man had said that he would be down early today and start taking over. Also, he'd said something about putting an ad in the papers for a steady assistant, and then going after some more business. *Thank goodness!* she mentally conceded.

The old standby accounts were paying the rent. But she agreed that a few new clients would help. She was really happy that Francis had definitely said the agency would do no divorce work. In this he was following Harry's ideas. Harry had believed steadfastly in the inviolable privacy of married people.

Then, too, Francis had said something about decorators. He'd really been pretty vague about this, as she thought of it now. Hattie smilingly realized that most of her new employer's conversations to date had definitely been on the vague side.

"Oh hell!" she said softly to herself as she stepped out of the elevator. "It'll all work out..."

As she rounded the corner of the hallway leading to the agency offices, she was brought to an abrupt halt by the line of men stemming from the agency door. They were six deep, but waiting patiently, in front of the door bearing the inscription: "MORLEY AGENCY—PRIVATE INVESTIGATIONS."

Why! she thought, dumbfounded, *there must be dozens of them!*

The air was filled with the leavening smoke of half a hundred cigarettes, but there seemed to be little conversation. A glance along the line of men waiting so patiently and the realization that most of them carried a morning paper, made Hattie know at once that Francis must have put that advertisement in the paper. Humph! An assistant, no less. And from the want ads!

Sniffing audibly and squaring her adequate shoulders in her smart suit, Hattie pushed her way through to the door behind which she could hear the phone ringing. The men near the door grudgingly gave way and allowed her to open it and get through.

As they started to push in behind her, Hattie, instinctively feeling the need for a little preparation for the coming onslaught, turned and announced in very positive tones that the office would not be opened for at least another half hour. Disregarding another forward surge and an unpleasant murmur from the mob, she managed to get the door closed again, and bolted it from the inside.

Darting to her desk, where she dumped her purse, paper, and a copy of a late novel which she was not to have an opportunity to open in the office, Hattie snatched at the jangling telephone. To an earnest inquiry about the "ad," she briskly replied that Mr. Morley would only interview in person and hung up. The instrument rang again at once, with an almost identical interchange as a result.

This continued for several minutes, until the pattern was broken by someone calling from Duke-and-Dixie's, demanding to know when Mr. Morley would see the samples. This was all a complete mystery to Hattie, but certainly a welcome relief. She promptly suggested that Mr. Morley would probably look at anything at ten o'clock. For a further change, the other party hung up first.

At this, Hattie simply took the receiver off the hook, and quickly fumbled open her morning paper. An ominous series of knocks and raps on the outer door had begun to add to the merry bedlam of the insistent telephone. The secretary of the Morley Agency thought that she had better get a look at that "ad," before going any further.

In days to come, when Hattie Campbell thought about this morning, she shuddered. Now, skimming through the extensive want ad section, she came almost at once to the notice over the more heavily printed name, "THE MORLEY AGENCY."

Lighting a cigarette for strength, she slowly and carefully read what was printed there, writhing slightly with each succeeding line:

YOUNG MAN WANTED—Rough tough, attractive; 25-30; 6 ft. or over; educated, ex-service officer preferred. "Man-of-the-World" type, single, unattached, familiar with weapons. Must be bondable for permanent employment as assistant to private investigator. Excellent salary plus private apartment. Good future to right party. THE MORLEY AGENCY

Lifting her eyes to the ceiling in silent prayer, Hattie could only murmur, "Oh brother," as she wearily put the phone back on its hook. There was an immediate ringing as the result.

At this moment, and just down the hall, Francis Morley stepped jauntily from the elevator. Slightly over medium height, he appeared to be slender; but to a knowing eye this slimness could be termed deceiving. More or less violently extreme sports clothes carried upwards the note set by the open sandals. He wore his hair in somewhat overlong but nicely waved blonde curls.

Francis Morley's features were fine, aristocratic and just a shade too regular. An unconsciously un-masculine something was hinted at by the play of brilliant blue eyes beneath his long and luxuriant lashes. The wide and handsome Morley brow, however, was at the moment a bit pale. This might have indicated a slightly hung-over condition. As he paced lissomely down the hall and approached the Agency door, he pondered briefly on this gay, gay city that offered so many opportunities for companionship. *Shouldn't have done it last night,* he mused, *this being the first day at the Agency and all.*

His line of thought was shattered as he turned the corner of the hall. The Agency was surrounded by dozens of restive men. All ages were here: young, old, fair and fat, well dressed and otherwise. All seemed to be hovering as if patiently waiting for something or someone. In a flash Francis realized that they had all come in answer to his ad, and were all probably waiting for him. Drawing himself up, he wedged his way through to the door, pausing only to give a haughty backward glance to some character who gave a low whistle. Fumbling out his key, he got it into the lock and opening the door, turned to the crowd: "I'm Mr. Morley. Now if you fellows will come in five or six at a time, I'll see you all as quickly as possible."

With a gay lift to his shoulders, he turned to face Hattie at her desk.

"My God, Bessie! It looks like the third act of *Aida* out there."

"Why didn't you tell me?" replied his secretary. "We could've had an agency weed out the applicants and you would only have had to see a few."

As about ten men had crowded into the reception room behind him, Francis fled into his private office, motioning Hattie to join him. This she promptly did, happy to get away for a moment from the din of the telephone. Inside, and with the door closed, Francis immediately went to the little closet washroom and mixed a hasty Bromo. The elderly secretary waited patiently by his desk.

When he emerged she smiled encouragingly and asked, "Who are Duke and Dixie, Francis?"

Early in their brief acquaintance these two had sensibly gotten down to first names; though, peculiarly, Francis often addressed her by such other names as came to mind at the moment.

"Duke and Dixie? Why?"

"Well, they called and said that they were to see you this morning. And so I told them ten o'clock."

"Oh, I know. The decorators. I've decided that we should touch up the place a bit."

"You'd better get with the boys outside then," Hattie indicated the outer office; "because they'll be here with samples in about an hour."

"Oh no!" Francis almost shrieked. "Hattie, I'm unwell this morning."

"Come, dear," laughingly purred the amused secretary, "pull yourself together. The show must go on."

"All right, Agatha. Put Duke and Dixie in the extra office when they get here." He paused as he inspected his sensitive and well-groomed hands, then continued, "I've got a dreadful hangnail..."

"Humph! I feel for you. What about this mob outside, to say nothing of the telephone going like mad—"

"All right, all right! Never mind the lash. I'll take care of the boys—one at a time, that is—and you get to the phone. Business as usual, dearie..."

As Hattie went back to her desk, Francis fitted a cigarette into a long holder, adjusted the shades at the window to a less penetrating glare, and sank resignedly into the chair behind the desk. Clicking on the interoffice communication, he said in a tired voice, "Okay. Send 'em in."

Chapter Four

One short hour later, Hattie at the reception desk was beginning to have a glazed look about the eyes. Between the still growing horde of applicants, and the continuous ringing of the phone, she was reaching a point just short of hysterical.

Added to the confusion were several more or less mad interoffice communications. And still the applicants seemed to come and go. The slight uproar in the outer office was calm and serene, however, in comparison to the present scene behind the door marked "Private."

Across the room from Morley's desk, and balanced at the top of a shaky stepladder, was a nondescript person clad in blue dungarees, run down half-Wellingtons, a striped Jersey in pink and green, and topped by a wild mop of mottled red hair. Seen from the rear, a definitely protuberant view, this person was holding up lengths of brightly colored draperies in either hand while muttering something unintelligible into the wainscoting. But these efforts actually had only a part of Francis' attention.

Squeezed into another chair behind the desk was a pert blonde manicurist, who was working deftly, though with an air of slight confusion, on one of Francis' hands. The hangnail, no doubt.

Added to the bright chatter of the blonde, and the mutterings of Duke (or Dixie—one couldn't be sure, really) on the ladder, the applicant seated before the desk began to show signs of increasing nervousness. He had just delivered a more or less idealized description of self and abilities, and had arrived at that conversational pause that requires something from the other party. Francis, who had decided "NO" at first glance, seemed to be actually more interested in the minor mystery of Dixie (or Duke).

At this point the intercom system brayed forth a frantic plea from Hattie.

"Mr. Morley, are we taking cases this morning?"

"Certainly, my dear. Business as usual." This last with a subdued titter.

"Please, sir, do hold still." This from the manicurist in an affected, lispy, little girl's voice.

The mutter from atop the ladder became a derisive snort, and a heavy voice mimicked: "'Please, sir, do hold still.' Get her!"

Right back came the very earthy natural tones of the handholder: "Up ye' bucket, Butch!"

The intercom chimed in with Hattie's "...and a Mrs. Bagnold wants us to find the Emir of Afghanistan—whoever that may be."

"Well for pity sakes, how did she lose him? Say, Hattie, do we trace missing persons?"

"Ya gotta missing link up the tree there," snapped the manicurist, rolling up her tools. "That'll be two-fifty."

Duke (or Dixie) started a hasty descent but became entangled in the yards of her draperies. From the midst of the entanglement came a threatening "Let me at that blondined Navy-bait..."

"Ladies! Please!" said Morley.

"She says that that will be satisfactory, and when will you see her?" came from Hattie.

"Yeah! You and who else?" came from one of the belligerents.

"What will be satisfactory?" demanded Francis.

"Mr. Morley, there is no need to raise your voice. You said 'two-fifty', and so I told Mrs. Bagnold that we'd be happy to locate the missing Emir—for two hundred and fifty dollars. And she agreed. She will be in this afternoon with the details."

The nervous applicant had begun to squirm, and seemingly unable to remain a spectator only, he burst forth with a peal of falsetto laughter. Leaning across the desk and patting Francis' arm, he burbled, "My Gawd, dearie! This is the gayest place in town. I'd just love to work here." Slumping coquettishly over the desk he leered inanely. "And I'll just bet that you and I could find lots in common…"

Repressing a shudder, Francis arose with considerable dignity. "I do not think, sir, that you are just the person. I wanted an ex-officer, someone younger, perhaps."

His meaning was very clear, and the rejected man also rose. Drawing himself up haughtily, he replied in his original curt tones: "Possibly I was mistaken, Mr. Morley. Certain types always want someone younger. As for myself, I'll have you know that I was a Lieutenant Colonel in the Air Force!"

Turning, he strode to the door with an air of offended dignity. He went out, followed by the manicurist, who winked at Francis in passing, and remarked, "Yah!—these fly-boys."

From the ladder, Dixie (or Duke) put in brusquely, "Well, Morley, what do you think?"

The fact that she obviously wanted an opinion on the draperies went unnoticed.

The harassed Morley flipped a key and said wearily into the intercom: "Hattie, are there many more?"

"There certainly are. Dozens! Also, will you see a Mr. Olsen?"

"What does he want?"

"He's with Chadwick Motors. We carry the account. Remember sir—'business as usual.'"

Resignedly Francis said, "Send him in."

From the ladder came a more frantic waving of the drapes. "Well, pal, what do you think?"

"I think I need a rest," the head of Morley Agency said.

The door opened to admit Tiger Olsen. Francis sat up in his chair, immediately interested in this newcomer.

"Well, let's do this quickly, a client is coming in. What was your school?"

The tall, well-dressed, and attractively large man smiled and said hesitantly, "Perhaps, Mr. Morley—"

"Please," he snapped, "allow me just a few questions first. Did you take a degree?" Francis looked over the two-hundred-pounds-plus of Olsen's development, noted the erect carriage, the good if slightly disarranged features, the excellent tailoring.

Amused, Tiger decided to play along. "Yes, sir. Arts—'44."

"In Service?"

"Captain, Marine Corps."

"Single?"

"Definitely."

"Well..." Approval began to shine in Francis' eyes. "Know the city?"

"Born here. Lived here all my life."

"Well, er, one moment." Flipping the intercom, Francis barked: "Hattie, please come in."

The door admitted the secretary almost at once. "Mr. Morley, this phone is driving me mad."

"Never mind that for a moment." Nodding at Tiger, relaxed and grinning in his chair, Francis asked, "What do you think of this one?"

"What do you mean?" asked a puzzled Hattie.

"Personally, I think he's just the type."

At this both Tiger and the secretary exchanged amused glances and burst out laughing.

"What the hell is so funny?" demanded Francis.

"Mr. Morley, this is Mr. Olsen—Mr. Tiger Olsen of Chadwick Motors."

Slumping in his seat, Francis moaned, "Oh, no!"

"Oh, but yes..." said Hattie. Then she turned to the visitor with something near hero worship in her eyes. "I remember, Mr. Olsen, when you came back. The parade went by just down below, and I frantically tore up paper and poured it out the window." Turning to Francis, she explained excitedly, "Mr. Olsen was a returned war hero."

From the top of the ladder came: "Say listen, you, never mind all that yak-yak. I can't stay up here all day."

Sizing up the situation, and in all modesty preferring to change the subject, Tiger asked Francis deferentially, "Mr. Morley, in my line I have had quite a lot of experience with custom upholstery. Now, may I make a suggestion here?"

"Why, certainly, please do. And my apologies, Mr. Olsen."

Turning to Dixie (or Duke), Tiger said, "I think that a rough copper drapery with maybe some metal in it would do well in here. Walls and woodwork of shades of light green, possibly some blue in it, but no yellow. The furniture in off-white leather, a darker green broadloom on the floor, bone-white desk, and one or two lamps with copper shades and so on."

"Brother, I wouldn't have believed it possible, but that's darn near perfect. You can come work for me, too, anytime ya' want to. How about it, Morley?"

"It all sounds grand to me. But first bring me in some samples in those colors, and we'll talk about prices. Am I free tomorrow afternoon, Hattie?"

"Not the way that mob out there is showing up."

"About four, then," said Francis to the decorator, who was bundling the draperies and ladder out the door.

"Maybe I can help you a little further," offered Tiger. Turning to Hattie, he said, "If you call Helen Roberts at the Preferred Answering Service—use my name—and ask her to monitor your calls, just putting through the actual business calls, and have her ask applicants to write, with their details and stuff, I think that she can get the phone company to make the switch in about an hour."

Heaving a sigh of anticipated relief, Hattie turned to the door.

"I don't know how I'll ever thank you, Mr. Olsen."

Then Tiger had a further suggestion. "If you would take all the names out there now, and route them back at five minute intervals, starting, say, at two o'clock, well, you could see about twenty every hour."

Overjoyed at this very sensible suggestion, Hattie went out beaming, with Francis' nod of approval.

Tiger turned to the man at the desk and said, "And now, Mr. Morley, if you have a few minutes to spare?"

"Mr. Olsen, you are out of this world! You can have all of my time that you want. But, what was it about?"

"It's like this," Tiger relaxed in his chair, as he went on. "I'd heard that you're new in Bay City, and I thought that perhaps sooner or later you'd be interested in a motor car. Now it appears to me that your business here is likely to be a very distinguished one. So, I don't feel that I'm at all out of line in suggesting that you consider one of our very distinguished cars. Our agency has the privilege of offering—"

At this point, his fine flow of sales-talk was interrupted, as—with uplifted hand—Francis asked, "Mr. Olsen, in a word, you are a car salesman?"

"That's correct, Mr. Morley."

"If you don't mind the personal note, this once—are you happy at it?"

"Well, sir, yes and no. The business has its ups and downs."

"Are you very sure that you wouldn't prefer to work on a steady salary basis, with, say, a year's contract as my assistant?"

"Mr. Morley, this is nice of you. It's a thing that I could consider."

"Mr. Olsen, I'll make you a proposition."

Looking Francis directly in the eyes, Tiger smiled wryly, and said, "That, Mr. Morley, is what I am afraid of."

Francis met the Tiger's glance steadily enough, though he did flush slightly. Then he continued, "There would be, possibly, some preconceived notions, about which I should have to disillusion you. The proposition that I have in mind is that I'll be very happy to purchase a car from you if it is your final sale for Chadwick, just prior to your coming to work for the Morley Agency at your own figure."

Hesitant, and aware of the fact that possibly his casual snap judgment might have made a bit of a fool of himself, Tiger replied, "I'll consider it, Mr. Morley. Now about this car."

Jumping to his feet, a more ebullient Francis gayly remarked, "Mr. Olsen, I'm just worn out here, though you seem to have straightened out most of my day for me. I thought perhaps that I would go and take a little refreshing exercise and then lunch. While you are considering my offer and I'm thinking about yours, wouldn't you care to join me?"

Tiger grinned. "That's right, there's nothing like a good workout. I'd be happy to join you. Where do—?"

Anticipating the question, Francis strode to the door. "I've discovered a perfectly divine ballet school, and only a couple of blocks from here."

Tiger blanched. "Did you say 'a ballet school'?"

"Yes, I'm sure you'll just love it. And you might be surprised."

The two men left the office, Francis pausing at the now more orderly reception desk to tell Hattie where they were going, while Tiger waited just outside the door.

Getting into the elevator, Tiger again shook his head, and muttered, "A ballet school..."

Chapter Five

After a short drive about the City, during which Tiger Olsen extolled the merits of his own Jaguar sports car in which they rode, Francis' insistent directions brought them to a rather down-at-heels building whose most prominent feature was a large and permanent sign—HALLS FOR RENT. At the entrance a display board listed, among other things, a "Personal" Get-Acquainted Club; Sanhedran's Gymnasium and School of Physical Culture; the Boros Toros Chorus of the Flamenco; and the Marie Antoinette Ballet Academy.

Tiger studied this directory as if seeking a last-minute reprieve, and finally, reluctantly, followed Francis' footsteps to the stairway.

"'You walks'," said Francis, obviously quoting an authority. "That's what they told me." Sizing up the big, athletic figure following him up the stairs, he added, "I'm sure that Sandy will be able to fix you with a costume."

"Well, look, Mr. Morley, maybe some other time—"

"Come on, don't chicken."

A resigned Tiger merely nodded his head and plodded on upward.

A dull door in a drab hallway, to which Francis had a key, let them into a small but well-appointed locker room.

Tiger was a bit surprised at this adjunct to a ballet school, but was by now determined to see this thing through.

"San-n-n-dy!" called Francis at the top of his voice. This brought in a wizened little character who looked to Tiger like the handler of a third-rate pug.

"Good morning, Frank, and why, yeah! It's Tiger Olsen." He put out a hand and pumped Olsen's enthusiastically. "We never met, but of course, I seen you around."

Francis interrupted, "This is Sandy. He owns the place. My, but you certainly seem to have contacts, Olsen."

"Yeah. Lots of people know me. Local boy, y'know."

"Sandy, have you got some stuff for Tiger? We want to do a little toe work."

"Sure, sure. Come around here, Tiger."

As he led the big fellow around behind some lockers, Francis called after him, "Bring him in when he's ready, Sandy."

"You betcha, Frank," came from an unseen corner.

Five minutes later he led Olsen, now clad in trunks and a T-shirt, into a fairly large gymnasium. Only a couple of men were present. One was working out on some weights in a far corner. And there was a flashy guy who looked to be a light, light-heavy punching a bag rhythmically and very expertly. He stopped as Tiger came in looking around for Francis.

The man at the bag, looking a bit top-heavy because of a well padded head and face protector, turned and came toward Tiger and Sandy, stopping to pick up another fighter's mask on his way.

"You're pretty good with that bag this morning, Frank," Sandy said. "Now, what's it gonna be with the Tiger?" Unaware of the big man's dumfounded confusion, the little trainer talked on as he led Tiger over to the padded ring. "Tiger's got about fifty pounds on you, Frank, but he looks—you'll excuse it, please, Tiger—he looks a little fat here and there."

"That's what I thought too," said Francis, "and a little muscle-bound. And besides, I've got a hunch that he can't box."

The embarrassed Olsen climbed after the others into the ring. At Morley's insistence he donned the protective headgear, while explaining that he had sparred around a little in college—but really hadn't done much boxing.

"Okay, Tiger, this is just for the exercise," said the amused Francis. "Let's try a couple of two-minute rounds. Time us, will you, Sandy? And listen, big man, I'm not expecting, so let's get it in there."

One and two-thirds minutes later, a bewildered ex-football player and all-around athlete looked up from where he sat, momentarily, in the center of the ring. He growled a bit truculently, "Kinda rough, aren't you chum?"

"That, Mr. Olsen, was for something you had in your mind. As far as you and I are to be concerned, I wanted to knock it out."

Getting to his feet and shaking his head, Olsen admitted, "Well, boy, that you did, and for sure. Why?"

Morley cut him short, "Aw, come on, slugger. Get in there and box. We both need the workout. Then, maybe, we'll go get that new car of mine..."

An hour or so later, in the offices of the Chadwick Motor Company, Francis passed over his check and received the pink slip that denoted his ownership of the snappy, underslung Jaguar at the curb. Smiling slightly and winsomely, the sales manager patted Tiger lightly on the shoulder.

"Nice work, boy." At Francis' amused chuckle, the manager explained, "Not many get 'em with the full price in cash these days."

Francis grinned wickedly. "Yes, I'm sure that you'll miss Mr. Olsen."

The Tiger cut in, embarrassed, but feeling that this should come from him.

"Sir, I hope that there won't be any hard feelings about this, but Mr. Morley has convinced me—that is, he has asked me to join his Agency as his assistant. And, well, I've agreed."

"Now look here, Olsen, if it's a question of more money—"

"No. No, sir. That's not it. It's just that I'm thinking that the work will be more interesting. Besides, the car business isn't too good right now... and, well, sir, you know how it is."

Resignedly, the manager admitted that he did know how it was, though in his own mind, and after a hasty appraisal of the two men, he was not entirely sure that he did. After some further conversation, Francis and Tiger were again out on the sidewalk.

"I think you'd better go down to the police department and get a license, or whatever, Tiger. By the way, what is your name, anyway?"

"Just Tiger will do nicely," said Olsen curtly.

"Well! That straightens that out. And while we're on the subject, you'd better call me Frank, when you feel friendly."

"Okay, boss. I'll go down and see Captain Starr, and then see you back at the office at two..."

Francis laughed. "Will Hattie be surprised! All those guys in this morning, and for nothing."

"Yeah, you'd better phone her and have her put a notice on the outside door that the position has been filled. And, say, you have her call Helen Roberts at the phone service, too."

Francis laughed again, and mincing a bit toward his new car, said, "Oh, I can see that you're going to be a big help to me. By the way," he paused, "I've already got a case for you."

"Yeah?" Tiger seemed a bit apprehensive.

"Yeah!" Francis said. "Butch, we've got to locate the Emir of Afghanistan for Mrs. Bagnold by five o'clock this afternoon. So there, you great hulk. Now get moving."

Glancing around to be sure they were unobserved, Tiger put a hand on his hip and flipped his other wrist.

"And whoops to you, too," he said with his boyish grin.

Chapter Six

It was the night before Francis and Tiger met and joined forces.

The long black sedan was parked near a dark corner beside a small park at the top of one of the city's hills. It had been there for only a few minutes, squatting ominously without lights, when a car pulled up across the street. After a moment a man got out of this second car and, looking nervously around at the dark and deserted neighborhood, walked across to the big sedan. As he approached, a rear door swung open and a lisping voice said, "Come on. Get in."

Almost reluctantly, the man climbed into the back seat of the big car.

The other occupant tersely demanded, "Did you bring it?"

"Now listen, Kay, this is a lot of money. I had to borrow—"

"Okay! Cut the crap, dearie! You had your fun, now you've got to pay for it. Give it to me."

"Well, first you give me the pictures, and the negatives, too."

Kay laughed bitterly. "Not this time. Come on, hand over the money. "

"What do you mean, 'not this time'?"

"I mean that this is only the first installment, and if you don't make your payments promptly, that invalid sister of yours and that boss of yours will each get a copy of that picture. Though, I can't say that they really do me justice."

The man started to protest angrily, and reached for the handle of the door to let himself out of the car. At this the hulking figure sitting in the driver's seat turned, quietly leveling a snub-nosed automatic at the frantic man behind.

"Get the money, Kay!" snapped Buster.

The protesting man leaned well forward, closer to the one in front, as if to plead personally with him. Before he could say a word, Buster's other hand reached high, and the descending blackjack hit the pleader expertly just behind the ear. He slumped limply in the tonneau of the car.

"Come on now, Kay. Get the money and hand it over."

After a moment, during which the young blond man fumbled through the inert one's pockets, he finally came erect with a thick envelope. Making sure that this contained currency, he leaned forward to pass it to his companion in the front seat.

Taking the money, Buster said, "Let's get him out of there. We'll drag him over onto the grass."

The two carried the man over into the park and dumped him limply beside some bushes, Kay gayly remarking, "My God, we always seem to be trundling bodies…"

As this sally went unanswered, the lissome youth bent to remove the unconscious man's wallet. As he started to rise with it in his hand, Buster shot him neatly between the eyes.

Moving swiftly, Buster put the gun in the hand of the unconscious man. Then, getting a finger on the trigger, he bent the unresistant arm so that the muzzle of the gun was pointed directly at the head of him who now held it.

Carefully squeezing the hand that held the gun, Buster again scored a neat hole in the head, though this one brought quite a piece of hair and brains out with it.

Buster walked away from the two stiffening bodies without a backward glance, moving quickly to the black sedan. The whole episode on the lawn of the peaceful little park had taken less than two minutes. The big black car sped away and into the city.

Not many blocks away, and on the same night, a bored and lonely-looking man sat drinking at the bar of Joe Cannelli's TROC. The barroom was deserted except for an obvious blonde who was obviously waiting for someone. Obviously anyone.

Conversation between the smirking, willowy, handsome bartender and the lone male customer was desultory.

"I've always heard that Bay City was really gay," the man offered rather pointedly.

As if he'd used a password, which in a sense he had, the bartender became at once effusively chummy.

"Well, my dear, it all depends on what you're looking for."

He leered toward the blonde along the counter with a questioning lift of an eyebrow.

"Oh, heavens no, not that," said the customer.

Both laughed shrilly in their quickly found intimacy.

"But where, I ask you, can one get a man?"

The nymph behind the bar pouted prettily. "Oh, the things you say, Nellie!" Then leaning forward confidentially, he rambled on effusively, illustrating each point with fluttering gestures of his hands and slim hips. "Of course, you can cruise the main drag—that's Market. You might pick up a serviceman."

At the customer's expression of distaste, the gay bartender went on: "Yes, they can be rough! So much dirt nowadays. Well, there's the Square. Always a lot of hustlers around there... but so shopworn, I always say... being pawed over on the bargain counter." He laughed shrilly at his own wit, then continued, "And there's the Baths, too. They're really best in the long run. Costs you a few bucks, my dear. But goodness! There are always two or three dozen there, and you can simply take your pick. It's the best go in Bay City I'm sure."

"But, aren't they all gay, too? In those places, I mean? I've never been in one."

"Well, yes," agreed the bartender. "Most that go there are. Of course, everyone wanders around stripped, and sometimes you can get so interested in something that you don't stop to consider the breed." Again the shrill, fluttery laugh. "But if you just ask for one of the house masseurs when you check in, they see to it that you really get something!"

"I'll bet," dryly commented the customer, finishing his drink. "I don't really know if I want a massage."

"Silly boy!" gurgled the man behind the bar. Writing an address on a bit of paper, he passed it over the plank. "Try this place. Just tell them that the bartender at Joe Cannelli's sent you."

Laughing again as the patron turned away eagerly, address clutched in his hand, the gay drink dispenser said gayly, "That one! 'Massage,' he says! I don't even think that joint has running water."

Chapter Seven

At police headquarters there was unusual activity in and about the homicide squad, with a good deal of it centering about the veteran Captain Starr. When his phone announced that Tiger Olsen would like to see him, however, the Captain briefly said, "Send him up."

A few minutes later Olsen came into the office and greeted the busy detective.

"Hiya, Tiger," returned Starr. "And what brings you here today of all days? If it's a parking ticket, I'll throw you out bodily."

"Whatsa matter, man," Tiger teased, "is crime on the increase?"

"Oh brother! And have I got a thing here. A suicide and a murder in the park, and no apparent reason for either one."

"Maybe you'd better hire a detective agency, huh?" laughed Olsen.

Starr bristled momentarily, then asked, "What's that supposed to mean?"

"Well, John, I'm going to work for one of the agencies— sort of a leg man, I guess. But I need a license, or permit, don't I?"

"What agency?" snapped the Captain.

"Morley."

"Oh, no! Tiger, not that character." At this the officer laughed hilariously. "Don't tell me you've become one of the boys?"

"Starr, I think you're wrong about that guy."

"My! It does sound like you two have gotten together at that. You sure surprise me, Tiger. Never thought you'd go that route."

"Look, Starr—" Olsen was obviously annoyed at Starr's implication. He went on: "Yeah, we got together. Down at Sandy's Gym. Morley knocked me on my ass twice in five minutes, just for thinking what you think."

"Oh, no! You mean that guy can fight, too?"

"That I do." Olsen rubbed his jaw reminiscently.

"Well, then, why the hell does he act—"

"I don't know, Captain," Olsen cut in. "Maybe it's some kind of Eastern gag. But he's okay with me, and I'm going to work for him. Now, about that permit, or whatever I'll need…"

Shaking his head in bewilderment, Captain Starr said, "Sure, Tiger. You have to furnish a bond with some bonding company."

"Yeah, I've got that. Had to have it when I went to work for Chadwick."

"And," continued the officer, "I suppose that you want to carry a gun, too?"

"I've got a permit and a gun," snapped Olsen.

"What!" gasped the other, "No mascara brush?"

Olsen grinned. "Boy, you're sure in a foul humor today. What's eating you, John?"

"The 'boys' again! I'm gonna suggest to the Commissioner that we have a special department just to handle the gay ones." Starr laughed abruptly. "Maybe your rough, tough Mr. Morley could help us out."

"Okay, okay. Who's done what to whom? Besides, I thought we had a vice squad," said Olsen.

"Oh sure, we've got a vice squad. Under Captain Morphy." Starr's tone was more or less caustic. "Morph's a good policeman. Thirty years on the force. Vice to him consists of three things: gambling, dope, and 'hoors'. He don't like all three, but he understands them. Now, since the war, we've got this new thing in Bay City. Everyone calls them 'gay.' We have gay bars, gay parks, gay clubs, gay theaters and hotels. In fact, I understand that there are even certain places that these guys can go and get serviced, at a price, with whatever they want."

"You mean... houses, like?"

"That's right," continued Starr. Then more seriously, "And it's all a matter of opinion whether these guys are criminals or not. We do keep special files on them, and records of their hangouts and so on. But sometimes you just don't know. They turn up in all kinds of places. We find two guys necking in a dark park. One turns out to be a commander in the Navy and the other a prominent attorney."

"Oh, no," laughed Olsen. "What did you do with them?"

"What could we do? We've got some younger judges these days, pretty smart guys, too; and tolerance seems to be the word. That pair was vagged, mostly so we could get them on the record. They were given thirty days suspended. After all, they were grown men; there were no minors involved; and what they were doing was probably anti-social, but hardly criminal."

Tiger shook his head. "Well, John, what is there about all this that has you so riled up today?"

The police officer leaned back more comfortably in his chair. "It'll be in all the afternoon papers, so I guess it's no secret. A man walking his dog early this morning found these two in the park—or rather the dog found them. They weren't hidden particularly, just off the sidewalk and near some bushes. One had been shot between the eyes, and the other through the head, as if he had aimed at his mouth. The gun that did both jobs was in this one fellow's hand, and a nitrate test showed it had been in his hand when fired. On the surface, a clear case of murder and suicide."

"No sign of robbery?"

Starr shook his head. "On the contrary; that was the first peculiar angle. One of these guys, a Kay Dunbar, had the other guy's billfold in his hand. It only had a few dollars in it. In his pocket Dunbar had his own wallet with about a hundred bucks in it. Both men had good watches and minor jewelry. The next question was what were they in the park for—or just on the edge of it, rather. The district prowl car went by that place about midnight—had their spotlight on all those bushes and the lawn. They weren't there then, though the doctor says that the shootings were at about that time. Another peculiar feature is that Parsons—that was the other one, Harry Parsons—had the gun in his right hand. His sister, with whom he lived, is an invalid. And she says Harry was definitely left-handed. He had polio once, and never completely regained the use of his right hand, though it looked perfectly normal."

"But what makes you think that they were 'that way'?"

"That's the rub. I told you that we have a pretty extensive file on these people. Kay Dunbar has been arrested several times, usually on a lewd-vag charge. This means that he was arrested in or about places, or with persons, in circumstances suggesting sex deviations. Once in a theater where some guy busted him in the nose for making advances. An usher called a passing cop. Another time in a raid on an after-hours drinking joint that caters almost exclusively to the boys. Now there's a new development with him: the medics report that he was on the dope. There was no narcotics notation previously. He seems to have had some money, but he was listed with us as an unemployed entertainer."

"Yeah," grinned Olsen.

"Parsons was arrested for writing a nasty invitation on the walls of the men's room in a park. He was automatically added to the files. Arresting officers at the time said that he broke down and admitted perverted practices. However, as he was not actually caught in an act, he was fined a few dollars for defacing city property. He had a very good job as chief accountant for a wholesale garment company. As far as we know yet, his accounts are all in good order."

"Crazy, man! Well, captain, I've got to be going. What does it all add up to?"

"Too early to tell you yet, but I've got a hunch this was murder both ways. You get sort of a feeling after awhile."

The men talked a little longer about the license for Olsen and came to a satisfactory arrangement. At the door, the football player turned, and with a grin said, "I still think you should consult a good detective agency."

"Say!" said Starr, his face unsmiling, "That might be an idea. An agency with a gay detective..."

Chapter Eight

Back at the office Francis had announced to Hattie that now she would only have to get rid of the applicants that were due to appear during the afternoon, as the job had already been filled. It was a minute before the secretary had taken this in. Then, as if recalled in a panoramic flash, all of the hectic morning came back to her.

"Oh, no! Francis! Not even someone who went through the mill?"

"Oh, but yes! Miss Campbell. Our new man is Mr. Olsen." Francis added with a smug titter, "And from the way you gave him the eye, I suspect that he's quite satisfactory with you, too."

"Bless you, boy. He's the handiest person we've had around this place since your late uncle."

"Well, dearie, don't get a gleam in your eye. I saw him first—or did I? Anyway, he'll move into the small office. Better get someone to put his name on the door. And, I do hope it's all neat and tidy—the office, that is."

At this point the outer door of the reception room opened to admit a haughty, mink-draped lady. She was preceded by a bust like the prow of a battleship. Coming to a stop in the center of the room, she blinked at both Francis and Hattie through a raised lorgnette before inquiring,

"And which of you ladies is Morley?"

Hattie nearly giggled aloud as Francis, in sepulchrally formal tones, replied, "I am Mr. Morley, Madame. You, I presume, are Mrs. Bagbones?"

The dowager snorted, then grinned. "Don't be fresh, young man. I am very nearsighted, and I made an excusable error. Yes, I am Mrs. Bagnold—and you are going to find my Emir."

With a significant glance at Hattie and then at the intercom on her desk, Francis maneuvered the buxom lady into his office. After being seated, Mrs. Bagnold peered around through her glass. "Humph! Not what I expected at all, young man. Thought you private eyes always had a bottle on the desk, and a long divan on which to—er—interrogate your female clients."

Francis had decided that this mad old girl had a very subtle sense of humor, and was actually enjoying herself. He played along, and in an entirely serious manner answered, "Madame, my secretary, Miss Campbell, whom you saw in the outer office, does all of this agency's drinking. My assistant, Mr. Olsen, who is unfortunately out at the moment, is definitely the ladies' aid. And now, Mrs. Bagnold, just where did you lose—er—the Emir?"

"If I knew that, young man—"

"Of course. Perhaps if we take it easier. The Emir, he is a stranger here in Bay City?"

"Why certainly! My sister sent him on from Rochester. She'd had him for a year, and I suppose that she'd just begun to tire of him. She wrote that he had begun to want so many things, and was even bringing his—er—lady friends home with him. But she fixed that!"

"Well, he certainly sounds like a charming house guest, and not one to get lost, either."

Mrs. Bagnold beamed in agreement. "Now that's what I would have said, too. We hardly had time to get acquainted. But he did have the cutest brown-pointed ears."

"Ah, yes, Madame. I'll get a detailed description in a moment. Perhaps a little more background, first. How old was his Highness?"

"Oh, quite young, but with such strong haunches. You know—that makes all the difference."

Slightly taken aback by this frankness on the part of his very first client, and quite aware of Hattie giggling in the outer office where she was raptly listening in on this peculiar conversation, Francis hastily agreed. "I'm sure that they do, Madame. Is there a possibility that the Emir has—er—accepted someone else's hospitality? Did he take his things?"

"Oh, dear no!" said Mrs. Bagnold, "I so wanted him to be happy with me. Then, for company, when I was not handy, there were the three Persian girls. They should certainly have kept him amused, now don't you think, Mr. Morley?"

"The three Persian—?"

"Yes! There are three, mind you. They live with me, too. But I just decided that we could all use a male in the house, end then my sister wrote about the Emir."

"It sounds ideal, I'm sure. Now, did the Emir speak to you before he left?"

"Well, we are more or less strangers, yet; though he spent a very restless night in my bedroom. However, everyone says that they do speak, quite plainly. And he did make some sort of loud growling noise when I unlocked the door this morning."

With some asperity, Francis suggested, "Perhaps, Madame, he didn't care to be locked in anyone's bedroom all night…"

Here Francis had the grace to blush, while wondering if all his clients would be so frank. "Perhaps," admitted Mrs. Bagnold. "But he didn't sleep a wink, just up and down the whole night."

"Well—er—yes, Madame. Perhaps I'd better have a more detailed description. If you can give me the Emir's approximate age, his height, weight, general features—"

"Frankly, Mr. Morley, I've been so busy, what with one thing and another, I really never took a very good look at him. I'm so nearsighted. And then, too, all these Siamese look alike."

Francis looked up suddenly from the scanty notes that he had made. Out of nowhere an utterly impossible thought had popped into his mind—impossible, of course. "Pardon me, Mrs. Bagnold, did you say the Emir was Siamese? I had understood you to say that he was from Afghanistan."

"Why of course he's a Siamese. That's only his real registration name—'Emir of Afghanistan.'"

Simultaneously with muted convulsive strangling noises over the intercom, it all became quite clear to Francis. As if to reassure himself, however, he asked—and in a menacing monotone—"Mrs. Bagnold, are we discussing a cat?"

"But certainly, young man."

"And I understand that he's a young Siamese, with cute brown ears, husky haunches?"

"Blue eyes," added Mrs. Bagnold.

"Blue eyes, just here from Rochester; and you have never really taken a good look at him?"

"Why, yes. That's—"

Francis rose and went to the door, which he opened unsmilingly. "Mrs. Bagnold, the Morley Agency always gets its man! It is now some past two. We will have the Emir at your home before five o'clock."

The lady also moved to the door, sensing, perhaps, the slight pique in which Francis found himself.

"That, young man, will surely be service."

"And may I suggest, Madame, that you leave your address at the desk, and, er, your check, if you please," Francis added as he courteously bowed the lady out and closed the door with a sigh of relief.

In a few minutes, Hattie entered following a perfunctory knock.

"Francis, I've got all of it on tape! If you ever feel dull or blue, I'll give you a playback." She was highly amused at the pained expression on Francis' face. "...and he was up end down all night," she murmured.

"Please, Minnie. I'm thinking."

"You'd better be thinking where the Emir might be."

"Oh, poo on the Emir. After a night locked in that old bat's boudoir, I doubt if he'll ever come back."

"Francis! You promised—and before five o'clock. And we do have her check for two hundred and fifty dollars."

"That's the point, dearie. Okay, here's what you do. Call some pet shops. You want a young Siamese, with strong haunches, brown ears, blue eyes—"

"Yes, Mr. Morley. I've got all that. And, y'know, most Siamese do look alike. They are either brown points or blue. But—"

"The old girl is blind anyway, and she said that she had hardly taken a good look at him. Besides, he was strange there, too; so I think that this will work. Get the beast sent up here, and when the Tiger comes in, I'll have him take it out."

"Okay, boss, if you say so." Hattie seemed a little dubious.

"I do say so. And, Hattie, this will show a neat profit for the agency for my first day. Besides," Francis laughed lightly, "according to all the stories circulating, what private eye is ethical, anyhow?"

The rest of the day at the Morley Agency was comparatively quiet. It was spent getting Tiger settled in his office, a job which Hattie—threatening to become a mother type—aided in as much as possible. Tiger left for the Bagnold residence, gingerly bearing a neat wicker traveling cage, with one Siamese meowing loudly within.

A very brief inspection had confirmed brown ears, blue eyes, and redoubtable haunches. The bored feline seemed to think fully as little of his viewers as they did of him. Much to Francis' surprise, even this unregistered specimen was worth seventy-five dollars, at least to the dealer who had sent him. However, being in no mood for a further discussion of cats, Francis had merely waved a glass casually over the lip-lifting pussy, and said, "Butch, I now christen thee the 'Emir of Afghanistan, the Second', and I advise you to watch the old gal after midnight."

Tiger had hardly gone on his way with the restive beast, when the phone rang. The connection switched to Francis, and he answered tiredly. To his complete surprise, it was Captain Starr of the Bay City Homicide Department.

"Morley? I'm sending a young lady over to see you."

"Well, that's nice. Whatever for?"

Francis was amused at the slightly belligerent tone of the officer when he said, "Now look, Morley, this office has a policy of always working with you private investigators, when and where possible. You people can often do favors for us, and in return we can often help you. Now this young lady is searching for her brother, who has been missing a week—"

"But, Captain Starr," Francis interrupted, "the agency, that is, Olsen and myself, we want to cooperate fully with the police. But I just don't see..."

"All right, all right! Let me tell it. Did Olsen tell you anything about a case that we discussed over here?"

"Oh, Captain, we're saving all that chitchat for bedtime."

"Now look here, Morley!" angrily exclaimed the officer.

Francis giggled, and then, more seriously, apologized for his joking. He continued, "Yes, Captain, he mentioned something about those two guys in the park."

"Okay, then, er, did Olsen tell you that our records showed—that is, er, what kind of fellows they were?"

"But of course, Captain Starr! What other kind of men would be found in each other's arms in a public park, even dead?"

"Please, Morley, I'm trying to be serious. And," the officer added reluctantly, "I think that we could very much use your help in this."

Francis recognized a quality in Starr's voice that would brook very little more foolishness. He decided to be serious.

"All right, Captain Starr. I will try not to imagine that there is anything personal about all this. You have two characters, shot in a park. Your records show that both were practicing homos—right?"

"Yes. Now that's..." the detective hesitated.

"Probably what you are trying to say, in your own coy way—and strictly impersonally, of course—is that you suspect that I, too, am a nervous type. Okay, think what you like, Captain," snapped Francis. "Now having cleared that much away, how can the Morley Agency assist the Police Department? And what has this woman's missing brother got to do with it?"

"That's what I'm trying to explain to you. You see, this, er, personality angle is way beyond my bunch over here. I don't have a man available who could possibly understand these people. I feel that, shall I say, that perhaps you do, er..."

"Yes, Captain Starr. Get on with it," Francis said grimly.

"So, here's the connection. If you came into this case as a private investigator, with a client, that is, and looking for the girl's missing brother, then maybe we could work together on it. I've got a hunch that this is all part of something big—like I told Tiger."

"But, Captain, I'm still not sure that I get the connection. This girl—"

"Oh, you didn't let me finish. You see, I know where Vivien Holden's brother is—"

"You what! Then why—?"

"Now, wait a minute. He's been in the morgue for four days, though I haven't told her so. The body was found in the surf, out at the beach. The face had been pretty badly beaten up, and there were some other funny details. I'll tell you more about that later. The point is, I want you to get all this before she arrives at your office. Aside from this other stuff, Art Holden had been shot by the same gun that killed those two fairi—pardon! those two guys in the park!"

Chapter Nine

Though very little more of Starr's call had made any sensible pattern, Francis had finally registered the idea that the detective captain believed that there was a series of murders, all somehow connected with crime based on vice, of a sort, here in Bay City. The officer had insinuated that perhaps a partial investigation of this murder-vice ring by the Agency could be more revealing than if conducted along the lines of official police procedure.

Francis admired the police officer's grasp of the situation, as well as his ability to visualize the most unorthodox use of the Agency. And, as he thought out the possible personal involvement in the matter, he mused, "This is certainly no Emir to contend with…"

At this point Hattie ushered a slight brunette, dressed in a becoming suit and wearing a smart fur piece, into his office. Francis, rising, smilingly indicated the comfortable chair before the desk, negligently flipping the intercom key to "open." He then walked to the window and adjusted the Venetian blinds slowly and carefully in order to give his secretary a chance to get ready to record whatever might be forthcoming. During this time and as he returned to his desk, he chatted lightly while covertly inspecting the client who sat tensely in the chair.

"Miss Holden, I'm sure that Captain Starr said it was 'Miss'?"

To this implied query, the girl, who was definitely attractive in a sort of regal fashion, merely nodded in reply.

As she seemed at a troubled loss as to what to say, Francis said, "I believe that Captain Starr said you were looking for your brother?" At the girl's nodded affirmation, he continued, "Well now, Miss Holden, it's not quite clear to me—why should the Homicide Department be interested in a Missing Person? There is, as I presume you know, a very efficient and complete department—"

Here he was interrupted by a rapid and evidently pent-up outburst from the pretty, dark-haired young woman.

"Mr. Morley, I've been just frantic—just crazy with anxiety since Arthur's disappearance—"

Francis deliberately raised a hand to interrupt. While her speech was swift and seemed to tumble out, it was obviously the talk and manner of a person of culture and refinement.

"Miss Holden, please, pardon me for just one moment, and let's take this easily..." He doubted, by the way her tiny, even teeth caught at her full red lip, that the girl would be able to discuss her affairs sensibly and quietly, but he hoped for coherence at any rate. "Just when did your brother—Arthur Holden, is it?—when did he disappear?"

"But that's the point, Mr. Morley," she replied with noticeable restraint. "It was almost a week ago. Arthur had been nervous and worried for several days. Then the bank had called about the overdraft—"

Francis again interrupted, partially to further calm and slow the overwrought young woman.

"I see. Now what exactly was it about the bank? I mean to say, aside from his nervousness, was this call the first indication that something was wrong?"

"Yes, yes!" she replied, and went on, "You see, we have several accounts. One is the estate's—we are orphans—" the client briefly interpolated. "And then there is a service account for actual expenses, and a general checking fund on which either of us may draw. But whenever we do draw on this account, we always tell each other; then, if it happens to be at a time before any regular dividend is due from the investments, we jointly transfer covering funds from the estate account to the general checking account." Here the young lady smiled fleetingly. Perhaps she had recognized Francis' delaying tactic for its kindly motive. In any case, she continued quite calmly, "I know all this is confusing, but it's really a part of it, to me; because it is all a reason why Arthur shouldn't have gone away. You see, the bank called to say that he had cashed a check for more than was actually in the account, and of course I told them at once that our jointly signed estate check would be promptly forthcoming."

Francis nodded in understanding, though he as yet failed to see where all this was leading. His smile, however, again elicited a like and charming demonstration from the client as she, now more composed, continued: "I spoke to Arthur that very evening and suggested we go to the bank together in the morning. I did not ask why he had drawn out such a large amount. I think it was thirty-seven hundred. Mr. Morley, please understand that he has a perfect right to the money, if he wishes. But anyway, he was moody and upset the whole evening, saying only that he would take care of it in the morning. Then he went to his room. I just happened to answer when the phone rang some time later. This person— it sounded like a very young man's voice, and then in a sort of way it didn't—demanded very rudely to speak to my brother. I thought perhaps that Arthur had gone to bed and I wouldn't like to disturb him, so I asked who was calling. Well, this man, or woman, was very insistent that I tell Arthur that it was a 'Kay Dunbar' calling. Of course, I went up to call him. We have a girl who comes in daily, but she leaves right after dinner, and this was almost eleven o'clock..."

For the first time, Francis nodded with some under-standing. The girl continued: "He seemed very excited when I spoke to him, and went to the phone at once. I remained upstairs, and so I heard none of their short conversation. But it was only a minute before Arthur came quickly up the stairs.

"I tried to stop him for a minute, asking if I could be of any help, but he only said roughly that he had to go out. I assumed he was going to meet this Dunbar person. A few minutes later, and again fully dressed, Arthur left the apartment."

Here her bravery momentarily deserted her, and tears glistened in her very attractive eyes.

"That was the last time in almost a week that I have seen him. I've been waiting for some word from him, every minute of the day and night. I've checked all the hospitals and contacted all our friends, and I've kept reading almost every new edition of the papers as they came out—" Here her rushing words came to an abrupt halt, and once again she was tensed and excited. "So," she continued, "this afternoon when the papers came and I read the little bit there was about those two men found in the park, and—well, there was that name, Kay Dunbar…"

Francis courteously handed her his handkerchief. The girl was really crying now. He made some solicitous and conventional remarks, adding, "And so now I see. That's why you went to the Homicide office?"

"Yes," the brunette nodded affirmation. "And the first man that I talked to was horrid. He seemed to think that I was enquiring about Dunbar, and he said some things about him that were absolutely bestial…"

Again Francis tried to soothe the distraught girl, and was partially successful. "I know, Miss Holden. Some of these cops are pretty rough. Of course, if your brother knew this man…"

His statement really demanded an answer, and after a pause, during which she wiped away her tears, the client nodded.

Very primly she said, "Yes, Mr. Morley. I do know about such things. I studied social services in college, and also did some contact work in an Eastern city. I became reconciled some years back to the fact that my brother has little interest in women, as such…" This she said bravely and unflinchingly. But as if in justification she added, "He isn't, however, the extreme type. There isn't anything particularly noticeable, or 'gay'—I think that's the common expression now—about Arthur. But all that could hardly be the reason for him to go away like this."

"Is there any possibility that your brother is, or was, being blackmailed by this Dunbar?"

The Holden girl brightened at this suggestion, but in a moment, as if she'd had the same consecutive idea that Francis had had, she was again obviously upset.

"That's what I thought, too. But—but then these men were both shot, and with a small automatic. And now Arthur has disappeared." Again the girl seemed near to hysteria.

Francis came around the desk and patted her heaving shoulders. In an effort to ease her tenseness, he softly promised, feeling a Judas as he did so, "Come now, Miss Holden, we'll find Arthur for you."

At this the girl's sobbing stopped. She raised appealing tear-drenched eyes to the attractive young man at her side.

"Oh, thank you. But there is something else. Can I, dare I, be completely frank with you, Mr. Morley?"

Francis smiled receptively. "I hope that you have been, Miss Holden."

"Yes, it's all true, what I've told you. But there is more. And I'm so mixed up, I just don't know who to trust."

"Please, Miss Holden. Whatever you tell me here cannot go any farther, particularly, if we are to locate your brother. The Agency should have every possible detail. Then, with the full cooperation of the police—"

At this last word, the girl again cried out. "Oh, no! Mr. Morley, I didn't tell Captain Starr quite everything."

"No, Miss Holden? Perhaps you'd better—"

"Will he have to be told everything I tell you, every detail?" she asked anxiously.

"Well..." Under the very peculiar circumstances, Francis hesitated. But with the mental reassurance that this whole conversation was being recorded, he continued, "Ordinarily, any information that an agency has from a client is 'privileged,' if you understand..."

"Yes, yes, I know," the girl hastily agreed.

"Except in a case of murder," Francis added.

At this last, the brunette blanched, revealing at least that her former remarkable coloring was natural.

Francis continued, "As there is no connection here between your brother's knowing Dunbar, and Dunbar's murder, I believe that I can safely say that Arthur Holden will, in consequence, suffer no further embarrassment."

Francis felt like a fraud and a cheat as he made this true if ambiguous statement, knowing as he did that Holden—in the morgue—was safely beyond any embarrassment.

The sister, however, was content to grasp at the hope of his words. In a more relieved tone, she said, "Oh, that's different, though I just don't see how it all fits in. You see, while I was talking with Captain Starr, someone brought in a small, tagged automatic and gave it to him. The Captain must have noticed me looking at it, for he briefly explained that it was the weapon used to kill Dunbar and that other person—" Here she hesitated again, as if still undecided.

"Yes?—and?" prompted Francis.

"That's what I didn't tell the police. That was Arthur's gun."

The girl had hardly finished with this revealing statement when Hattie interrupted to tell Francis that Mr. Olsen had returned. Asking that his assistant be instructed to join him, Francis explained to his client that the Agency staff would start at once on an extensive search for her brother.

At this point, Tiger came into the private office. After introductions had been made, Francis suggested that he see Miss Holden to her apartment, and while there perhaps get some further details about the missing man. He assured the young woman as she was leaving that he had complete confidence in his assistant's discretion, and suggested that she could feel free to tell Olsen anything that might help in locating her brother. Francis purposely did not tell Tiger of his own knowledge of the brother's whereabouts; feeling that without the knowledge Olsen might glean even more pertinent information.

This Tiger seemed to be well on the way to doing as he left with his charge. Smiling infectiously and with a suitable light conversation, he was already charming the petite brunette as they turned to leave the Agency. However, just as Tiger and the pretty client were at the door, the brunette turned suddenly to Francis.

"Mr. Morley! I just remembered! The diary! Arthur has kept a diary for years, at least he used to. When we were smaller he sometimes read it to me." She sighed, at the memory. "It's been some years since I've actually seen it, or since he has mentioned it, but I do think that he still keeps it. Perhaps if I can locate it among his things—"

"That would be fine," Francis said enthusiastically. "If you do find it, please bring it right in," he urged, but without much hope that if found it would be of any help.

As the outer office door closed finally on the pair, Francis dropped onto a divan in the reception room. "My beads, dearie! What a day! Did you get all that in there, Hattie?"

"Certainly. It's on tape for posterity," said the secretary, pointedly looking at her watch. "Mr. Morley, it's just now past six. When would you suggest that we close the office?" she added with the tone of an overworked employee.

"Well, Minnie, from the look of things I'd say that this laundry was on a twenty-four-hour shift. Okay! Transfer all calls to the phone service. I'll call 'em later and let 'em know where I am. And you, you go straight home, dearie. Never mind those big Marines on the streets," he added lightly.

"Yeah? Well that goes for you too," gayly replied the secretary, though she blushed furiously as she said it.

"Well!" Francis softly exclaimed to himself, "First the Tiger, then that one. Could be my slip is showing..." He grinned roguishly as he picked up the phone to call Captain Starr at the Homicide Bureau.

Chapter Ten

Captain Starr stolidly eyed the group of men gathered in his office. Despite the lateness of the hour and regardless of the fact that their conversation, with many interruptions and developments, had already lasted over three hours, those present appeared to be alertly interested in the summary the Homicide officer now offered. The only dissenting note came as an occasional scowl from the graying, paunchy man who sat beside Starr behind the desk. This man had been introduced to Francis as Captain Morphy, the head of the Bay City Vice Squad.

Even at the outset, and with a witheringly casual inspection of the agency man, Captain Morphy had been openly and scornfully hostile. Mouthing a large cigar, he had barely repeated Francis' name upon Starr's introduction, and was at once slightly dazed as Francis gushingly remarked, while giving a flashing display of limp-wristed gesture: "Oh, Captain Morphy! And of the vice squad! Well! I've certainly wanted to meet you."

"Yeah?" Morphy, cigar clutched in a ham-like fist in mid-air, stood open-mouthed.

"Dear me, yes!" Francis giggled coyly. "It seems we have so many friends in common."

Morphy turned threateningly to Captain Starr: "What the hell is this, a gag?"

Even the taciturn Starr was amused, but he placatingly nudged the vice officer into a seat next to his own. His glare at Francis had a twinkle, as he brusquely said, "Okay, Morph, you're being kidded. And you too, Morley—knock it off."

The men present then discussed the situation for some time, until the phone announced another, and expected, visitor. This man proved to be the lonesome one who'd been guided on his gay way by the bartender at Joe Cannelli's TROC bar. He was evidently known to the officers, who greeted him with respect. Captain Starr explained to Francis that this gentleman was representing "another government agency," was interested in the narcotic traffic, and that there now seemed to be some tie-in with these three murders immediately occupying the local attention.

And so, then, these four—with occasional accessory officers who came in to offer pieces of information, surmise, or facts—had conferred to the point where Captain Starr had offered his summary of the matter.

"All right, then. Now as far as we know at this time, we have that gun, and we know that the first to die, Holden, was its owner. Now there appears to be some evidence that Holden was being blackmailed. Incidentally we've got to check with the officers of the bunco squad in the morning to see if we have any extortion reports that may tie in here. To get back to Holden, he seems to have been either worried or scared. Then he got together nearly four thousand dollars and, at a call from Dunbar, went to meet him. It is probable that he carried the gun and the money with him. He next appears washed up on the beach—two days later, without either the money or the gun. He had been very badly beaten about the face, but he had been killed with a bullet from the gun."

Here Francis interrupted, "Which came first?—the beating or the bullet?"

Both police captains glared at Morley, but Starr patiently answered the question.

"The morgue lab seems to think that he was shot first, then beaten afterwards. Maybe the idea was to destroy his identity."

"Okay," Francis said, "I only asked."

"Sure, sure."

"Now here is where it may all be guess work. It is the expressed opinion of Holden's sister that her brother was 'one of the boys.'" The homicide officer glared around to assure himself that he was understood. "And as there is no other apparent connection, it is possible that he was being blackmailed because of some such activity. Now, this is partially confirmed by the fact that his last known contact seems to have been Dunbar, who had a long record of active if petty homosexuality. Also, Dunbar must have been in some racket that paid off, because he didn't work and always had plenty of spending money. But—and in this connection—Dunbar had also become a narcotics user during the past year.

"Now, when these two subsequent, er, men were found murdered—and we are quite sure that both Dunbar and Parsons were murdered, and by the same gun that had killed Holden—we of course put out the usual pick-up order on all known associates and similar vice characters. This was with the help of Captain Morphy..." this last with a placating glance at the still disgruntled vice-squad leader, "...and, while we got nothing that has as yet seemed pertinent to these three killings, we do find that of the 'gay' boys arrested, there are now over twice as many 'users' as there were in a similar pick-up a year ago. This, I believe, is also checked out by another set of records."

The narcotics agent nodded in agreement and Starr continued, "And so it begins to look like we have several connected problems on our hands. First, we have three known killings. Then, we may have an organized blackmail racket. I forgot—it looks like Parsons, the guy that got it with Dunbar, was being blackmailed, too. And now, we have a narcotics distribution; and this seems to be tied in with the people in this 'gay' group."

Here the federal man put in a word.

"Believe me, gentlemen, from the size of this distribution, as far as the narcotics are concerned, this is big business. One thing puzzles me, though, Captain Morphy. Why does Bay City have such an overlarge percentage of these queer people? They seem to be actually encouraged here. Why, with their own clubs and bars. Well, I may be old-fashioned, but I just don't get this local tolerance."

Francis sniffed audibly, then said, "I seem to recall that several hundred federal government employees have been loudly bounced in Washington lately, and for just such little peccadillos…"

Morphy, the vice-squad officer, shook his head wearily.

"Yeah. And sometimes I don't get it either. Y'see, this town used to be wide open. It was the talk of the world, being a seaport and all. Things were pretty much under control, and everyone was making a little money. Then these people that always want to clean up everything— well, it seems that after they lost out on prohibition, they decided to run all the 'hoors' out of town. Finally, we had to close up all those quiet, friendly, well-regulated houses…" The officer sighed reminiscently.

"Sounds cozy," murmured Francis.

The policeman ignored this, and continued: "This put all the girls on the streets and hustling in bars, unregulated and uninspected, too. Even this didn't satisfy the 'do-gooders.' First we had to run 'em off the streets; and now it's outa the bars, too. I dunno. This is a sailor's town. It was once a great port. I guess these young fellas today just gotta do something with the time on their hands."

As the vice officer paused, the federal man asked, "But why all these open 'fag' bars and joints?"

"Oh that's pretty simple to explain, I guess. Personally, I always want to plant a foot in those cuties' butts, but the new Commission has psychiatrists now who advise that these people should be allowed to congregate in their own places. I suppose that it does eliminate a lot of possible friction—fights and stuff that might get started in regular joints. Yeah, and it does make it easier for us in a sense, 'cause we can keep an eye on them better. For their own protection, too. Some of them are mighty big taxpayers."

The government agent shook his head. "It still doesn't make sense to me, though they tell us some of the same things. I guess they could be right: these people aren't actually criminals."

Francis snickered audibly at this.

Captain Starr hastily brought the discussion to order with a terse, "It certainly looks like this gang we're dealing with are criminals; and we've got to get to them fast. Now, gentlemen, this is my idea: Mr. Morley here is practically a stranger in the city. He is, incidentally, a licensed operator of a private agency. He, er, that is, well, ahem, he wants to cooperate with the department. And as he has every appearance..." Starr bogged down for a moment, actually blushing, and distinctly at a loss for words.

Francis, for the first time during the conference, abandoned his flippant attitude and took up where the captain had paused.

"Gentlemen, let's face it. Suppose we put it this way, and stop mincing words..." Strangely, and surprisingly to his listeners, his words were now clipped and sincere, and his tone distinguished by a dangerously steely quality that they had not heard from him before. "Our immediate target seems to be a gang, or organization, that blackmails and dopes the 'boys.'"

Turning to the government agent, Francis continued, "I understand from what you said before that you tried to work your way into a few places, but just didn't seem to fit. The point here seems to be that I look to be more the type, and can probably crash this outfit somewhere. I'm willing to try to find out where the racket centers and where the stuff is pushed. As I see it, there must be some central spot. And the question is—where is it?" Francis looked around at the three officers questioningly, but received no answer or comment. "All right, now here is a thought that came to me when Captain Starr told us about Holden. If he was shot first and beaten later, this all must have taken some time. Were his clothes bloodied, Captain Starr?"

The homicide officer shook his head. "I'd say no to that. The body had been in the surf for some time, but as I recall there were no bloodstains on the collar of his white shirt."

"Well, gentlemen, maybe he had his shirt off," mused Francis. "Anyway, as I see it—where was Holden killed? That might be our spot. Now I suggest that we all go down and take another look at the late Mr. Holden and his things. Maybe with these angles one of us will get a new idea. What do you say, Captain Starr?"

Chapter Eleven

High on a hilltop overlooking the city whose lights twinkled in a many-colored magic carpet beneath them, Vivien Holden and Tiger Olsen huddled closer in the sleek little sports roadster. During the several hours since they had soberly left the Agency offices, the couple had become happily and closely acquainted.

The big ex-Marine had certainly made many conquests in his comings and goings about the Bay City; but what had started as simply a tactic to take the beautiful girl's mind off the problem of her missing brother had swiftly flowered into a more personal thing between the two of them. They had had a leisurely dinner in a quiet out-of-the-way spot, during which the attractive young woman—who at times hardly seemed more than a girl—had retold much of what she had already given to Francis Morley. This time, however, and with her listener holding her hands in his own, her narrative had been without tears. She felt, somehow, that this brutishly big man who listened so quietly and attentively to her hesitant fears about her brother, his character and his peculiarities, was a protection—a sort of buffer between those false values and a real understanding between a man and a woman. Also, and as if to prove her own normality, she had welcomed his increasing personal interest and contact.

Suddenly it seemed to come to both of them, seated here above the brightly illuminated city. Here was a peace of mind and mutual regard that demanded an even closer, more intimate, expression. The brawny arm about Vivien's shoulders now pulled her roughly but tenderly to a welcomed masculine embrace. As their lips met, seeking and tentative, Tiger could feel the thump of his heart beating against the firm out-thrust breasts of the girl in his arms. As her now feverish lips worked on his own, and her questing tongue sought a reply against his teeth, the big healthy man felt a surge of desire pass through his trembling body that demanded only one thing.

Even as her busy tongue found his, his big hands tenderly encircled her offered breasts. Here, too, he thought in a flash, was a firm erectness burning to be satisfied, an erectness that matched the burning within his own loins. At once Tiger knew that all the many experiences of his life— and the stalwart man's opportunities had been many and varied—had been merely training for what this night might bring. With a soft reluctance he pulled his lips from her demanding mouth and, tenderly kissing her passion-fevered eyes, murmured, "Oh, God! Vivien, darling... we must!"

With a complete understanding of the man's need, she swayed away from his embrace and, bringing her own taut emotions under control, replied pantingly, "Yes, Tiger. Yes! Tonight—now! My place isn't far, and I'm sure that Arthur won't have returned..."

The mention of the missing man seemed to have broken the spell that was on them. With a short husky laugh, and a last hasty kiss on the tip of her pert nose, Tiger started the car.

Almost two hours later, the dream-like quality of their ecstasy was shattered by the insistent ringing of the telephone. Clasping the woman tightly in his insatiable embrace, Tiger whispered into Vivien's ear, "Darling, let it ring... let it ring..."

But after another long and passionate moment surrendered to his demands, which were no more or no less than her own, she pulled away from his arms.

"No, Tiger... No! Wait, oh, dearest, please wait. I must answer. It might be Arthur..."

He released her reluctantly, as common sense intruded into the magic whirlpool of their coupling. He grunted wryly and snorted, "Huh! Probably a wrong number..."

The girl, turning back the quilt under which they lay, switched on a soft bedside lamp. Searching about the foot of the very disturbed bed for the dressing gown that had been summarily removed from her, she finally located the garment.

As she rose to put it on, Tiger was again amazed with the tiny, almost fragile appearance of the perfect body, a body whose strength he now knew could equal his own in its demands. Watching her as she left the dainty, feminine bedroom, he sighed with satisfied repletion at just the memory of what they had so recently had for each other. He closed his eyes and slid down into the bed, enjoying in anticipation the further pleasures to come.

Vivien's voice brought him rudely to his senses. Again she stood in the doorway, fists planted comically on her hips and laughing unreservedly. Her unfastened robe hung negligently open, renewing Tiger's pleasure.

"It's for you, ya big lug. I think it's your boss."

With a long sigh, Tiger climbed out of the bed and started toward her, unaware and unashamed of his rugged nakedness. Encircling her with his arms, he lifted her up so that their lips were joined in a kiss. He held her so, her feet off the floor and with all of her lithe body pressed molded to his own. After a moment she pulled her head away, laughing.

"The telephone, stupid. This can wait…"

"Oh, no it can't," he murmured as he nuzzled hungrily at her throat.

Still holding her firmly against himself, he lowered her slowly and gently, their warm sweating bodies sliding easily against each other. For a moment, Vivien, too, was almost carried away by his urgency. But as her toes neared the floor she managed to pull herself away from his stiffening desire.

"Hey, you've got to answer the phone. It's Mr. Morley…"

Releasing her, Tiger resignedly turned down the hallway to the telephone. Behind him, and with a gay and promising laugh, Vivien happily turned back to the bed.

Picking up the instrument, Tiger said, while suppressing a yawn, "Yes, boss?"

"Well, me good man, did I disturb something?" Francis chuckled.

"Huh! You have been reading, maybe, too mucha the Spillane. We were just discussing Arthur," replied Tiger.

"Oh yeah? Well, never mind that now. Did you find the diary?"

"Uh, well, y'see, boss, we just about got here, and…"

"Yes, dear. Mother knows! Now listen, get your clothes on…"

Tiger flushed—for the first time actually aware of his complete nudity. He laughed shakily as Francis continued: "You and I are going night-clubbing."

"Oh, Frank! Tonight?"

"Yes, lover man, tonight! We're going to look for a party."

"Boss," Tiger laughed, "I've got a party—"

Francis broke in, "Tiger, this is serious. We've got to find some people, and we can't waste any time at it. So, come on. That'll keep. And I'll meet you outside the Bait Room."

"Oh, now boss! Please! That's one of those swish joints."

"You'll be safe, dearie. I'll protect you. And besides, I doubt if any of them could do much good with you tonight..."

Tiger laughed. "Boss, you were never more right. Okay, give me half an hour."

Quickly replacing the phone, he strode back toward the bedroom mentally calculating: *fifteen minutes to dress and get there. That gives me fifteen minutes more here...*

Actually, Tiger was fifteen minutes late.

It was some time before this phone call, however, that had found Francis and the three officers in the Bay City Morgue.

Spread out on a worktable before them were all the personal effects of the late Arthur Holden, whose body they had just examined. The suit of clothes, though soiled and salt-stiffened from its time in the ocean, was of obvious quality—as were the shirt, shoes, handkerchief, socks, and so on. Here, Francis mentally catalogued the usual men's attire.

"Is this everything?" he asked.

"The works," glibly answered the attendant.

Francis insisted: "No wallet, papers, jewelry—anything like that?"

The morgue man only shrugged, and indicated the coarse manila envelope whose contents—a case of keys, a single long flat key on a rubber band, a pair of cuff links, and a tie clasp—were spread out before it.

"Do you remember what pockets these were all in?" asked Francis.

"Why, yes. It happens that I received him and I do." The attendant hesitated, then explained, "Y'see, we usually go through all the pockets and check for jewelry the first thing."

Captain Morphy snorted. "Yeah! I'll bet."

The others grinned, and, a little vehemently, the morgue man insisted, "Think what you like, but this is all that was on him. Say, I remember something funny, though. This key on the rubber band, it was shoved way up on his arm, up past his elbow."

Examining the key more closely, the narcotics man suddenly exclaimed: "Say! I've seen this before, or rather, one just like it. You remember I told you that I went to the baths? Well, they give you a key like this for the small room that you get. It's got a bed and a chair and some hangers for clothes. You're supposed to put the towel they give you around yourself and then you wander around." He paused, momentarily flushing at the recollections that came to him.

Francis broke the brief silence by exclaiming excitedly: "That's it, then!"

"That's what?" demanded Captain Starr.

"That must have been where he was killed! Look, Captain, don't you see what is missing here?"

Both of the detective officers again looked over the scattered garments. Then Starr answered, "Why, sure. His watch, billfold—"

"No, Captain. No!" Francis interrupted. "I mean his underwear. Shorts, maybe... and a T-shirt, or something. Where are they?"

Involuntarily they all turned to the morgue worker. Sensing their question, he shook his head.

"Uh-uh. He didn't have any on. Just what you see there."

"Well, then, can't you all see it!" exclaimed Francis. "He was stripped when they shot him, with just that key on his arm. Then, when they dressed the body to take him out, they just put on the outer clothing, not bothering with the skivies—or the necktie. Look, no tie there," Francis indicated the table. "But there's a tie clasp. Don't you all see it?"

The homicide chief nodded, though hesitantly, and turned abruptly to the federal man.

"Where is that joint? We'll take it apart!"

Again, Francis interrupted: "No, Captain. Not that way. I've got a better idea. Suppose I get a party together and take them all to the baths after the bars close. That way Olsen and I can look the place over thoroughly. You can always shake it down afterwards."

The officer agreed that this would be a better idea.

Francis grinned as he turned to Captain Morphy and asked, "Where would one of the boys from out of town go to meet some characters? I mean a nice place, 'gay' but refined... expensive?"

Unhesitatingly Morphy replied, though he looked his disgust, "The fairies with dough seem to hang out at the Bait Room. That's a joint over on Broadway. They got a bunch of the boys in the floorshow, all dressed up like women..."

Francis laughed, and even the other two men smiled at the vice officer's expression as Morley, looking completely innocent, asked, "Honestly! Do they, Captain Morphy? And which one of the chorus is your favorite?"

The stolid officer pondered this a moment before replying. "There's one there, calls himself the King of the Queens. Now he's real pretty—"

The Captain broke off with an angry string of obsolete curse words at the amusement he saw on the other faces. When he had exhausted this vocabulary, he added belligerently, "Well, you asked me..."

"Okay, so I did," smiled Francis. "Now, let me get at a phone."

As he searched through a small memo book for Vivien Holden's number, Francis added rather cryptically, "I'll just take along my own rough trade, though, instead of trying the house product..."

Chapter Twelve

Francis and Tiger met as planned, in the convenient parking lot adjoining the chastely designed but brightly-lighted exterior of the building that housed the Bait Room.

Francis, who had come by cab, paced restlessly up and down as he waited. He had a partially formed plan in his mind by the time Tiger pulled up in his Jaguar. A good deal of Francis' light and disdainful manner had obviously been discarded as he greeted his assistant.

"You're late, Olsen," he snapped, and then removed the sting with, "Probably held up in a good cause, though. Park over there in the corner and let's talk a minute..."

After they were comfortably seated in the parked sports car and Olsen had briefly reported that Vivien Holden was safely at home, Francis inquired, "Did she find that diary?"

Tiger flushed. "Well, as a matter of fact, we never did get to look for it. Y'see, after we'd had dinner—"

"Tiger, please, listen to me," interrupted Morley in tones more serious than any Olsen had heard from him previously. "This is serious, and to all concerned. To me, to you, the Agency, the police, and even to Vivien Holden. You see, Arthur Holden was murdered. I've just come from the morgue, where I saw his body. Now, here's the story, or part of it. There have been three murders that the police know of, a lot of blackmailing, and a busy narcotics ring. And there's almost nothing to go on about any of it. Now, because of the peculiar setup, the police—your Captain Starr, at any rate—think that the Agency can help them in this. I might add that federal authorities are already mixed up in this as well. Do you begin to get the picture?"

"Yeah, Frank. I see what you mean. But where do we come in?"

"Well, among the few things that we do have to go on is the fact that all these people are 'gay,' homosexuals."

"Yeah, I follow you."

"There must be some contact in one of these joints they hang out in, like maybe the Bait Room here. Now, another thing. Holden was possibly killed in a gymnasium or in a bath house—or in one of those so-called Turkish Baths. I'll tell you more about that later on. There are a couple of other leads that point the same way. There are five of these 'baths' in the city. One is entirely respectable; one is questionable; and the other three are definitely 'gay' houses."

"Okay, boss. So let's go take a bath."

"It's not as easy as that, Tiger. I am hardly known here, but you are. Now, I figure that if we make some of these joints tonight and pick up a small crowd as we go along, we can all end up in one or more of these baths by morning. That way, it will all seem very natural."

Tiger interrupted. "Look, Frank, and don't misunderstand me, but don't you think that I might look a little out of place?"

"Uh-uh! That's the idea. I'm supposed to be a wealthy young thing from the East who has picked you up. This way we can be partially sure of not being bothered by any of those guys. And besides," he added with his former twinkle, "I'm sure you'll attract a crowd."

After a long and caustic look at his employer, Olsen said, "The crowd had better not crowd me."

"I know, Tiger. But look, no rough stuff if you can help it. These people tell everything to each other, and the word would get around too soon if you got too rough. Please take it easy. Okay?"

After a very little more conversation, the two men went into the Bait Room.

This was actually a long barn of a hall, exotically hung with draperies and very dimly lighted except for the stage at one end and the bar at the other. The space in between was crowded with many small tables, which seemed to be all filled though it was past midnight. Among the guests were very few women. Most of these were either more masculine in appearance than many of the men about them, or they were part of the several large parties of obvious sightseers.

On the stage, a man dressed as a woman in a costume that displayed oversized and obviously false breasts sang a song about "My military man... he marches on my front..." and so on. This was done with much eye rolling and a few burlesque bumps and grinds. While the very professional performance was wildly received by the audience, the entertainer had neither much of a voice nor much personality other than the two outstanding projections.

A headwaiter led them toward an empty table. On the way, Francis, who had again adopted his gayest manner, even to a slightly mincing step, loudly remarked, "My Gawd, dearies! There's nothing like this in Philadelphia."

Then, he pointedly asked their guide if this went on all night.

"No, sir." This with an understanding smirk, and an appreciative glance at the embarrassed Tiger, who followed. "We stop the service at two o'clock, though sometimes they just sit and camp until three or four," he gushingly confided.

"Well!" exclaimed Francis. "We're out to make a night of it." He slipped the man a folded bill, and added, "Though I would like to meet some of the local girls."

The attendant acknowledged the tip with a smile and said, "Perhaps we can fix that for you, too."

As their orders were taken, Francis and Tiger looked the place over carefully. A cleared space at one side and along the wall seemed to lead to several side doors. Three of these, in a row, were spotlighted, and labeled, "Men," "Women," and "US."

Francis pointed out some other less conspicuous doors to Tiger, remarking that he was curious as to where they might lead.

After disposing of several drinks, and being entertained by further gaudy impersonators, none of whom were particularly amusing, Tiger rose, excusing himself. Francis quickly suggested that he might blunder into one of the unmarked doors to see what he could see. With a nod, Olsen weaved off through the crowded tables to the men's room, attracting many roving eyes as he went.

Several persons spoke, casually inviting him to sit down for a drink. Some, more bold, suggested other things. Grinning fatuously and shaking his head, Olsen kept on his way. One or two obviously interested men evidently decided that they should powder their noses just at this time, and followed the big man closely. Because of these, Tiger was forced to turn directly into the washroom, where he hastily locked himself in a cubicle. His thoughts, as he paused there, were mixed. In a way—this was all very funny. Laughable, at least.

And then he thought of Vivien. It occurred to him suddenly that she as yet didn't know of her brother's death, and the presentiment came clearly that he would probably have to be the one to tell her. With this grim prospect foremost in his mind, he ignored the appraising glances, leers, and tentative conversational bids that were directed at him when he left the cubicle. He washed his hands and stalked out of the men's room.

He actually did inadvertently turn in the wrong direction, and passing one of the questioned doors, noticed that it was slightly ajar. Quickly making up his mind, he assumed a slightly drunken swagger and lunged into the lighted room, which appeared to be an office. Moreover, the surprise of finding an old acquaintance behind the desk, left him momentarily speechless.

"Tiger! Where did you come from? And what are you doing in this joint? Didn't think you'd go for the boys," remarked the grinning man behind the desk.

Tiger flushed and then laughed defensively as he stammered, "So, this is where Joe Cannelli makes all his dough…"

He stared, drunkenly, about the spacious and well-appointed office, noting that there were several other doors besides the one through which he had blundered. Recalling his role, he thickened his speech a bit as he added, "Yeah, showing a pal from the Marines some of the town. He wanted to see everything. Your joint, Joe?"

"Well, I run it. I have some partners, though. We gotta lot of connections."

Rising, the heavy-set, foreign-looking club operator indicated a small well-stocked bar.

"How about a drink with me, Tiger?" As he mixed the suggested drinks, he asked casually, "This friend, anyone I should know?"

"Nah! This guy is, or was, just an old buddy. He's been living back East..." As Tiger improvised he had the beginnings of an idea. "Say, Joe, this is sure better liquor than we got out there."

Cannelli laughed. "It better be. It isn't cut."

Tiger laughed with him, and after another gulp of his drink, said, "I haven't seen this guy for some time. Well, I always thought he was a little different. But I don't know. Anyway, I suppose we'll make a night of it. He says he wants to try everything from sarsaparilla to a shot in the arm."

"Huh! Sounds like an expensive night."

"Oh, this guy's loaded. Say, Joe, where are some really rugged joints, where these guys go? I've been going with girls so long, guess I don't really know my way around the town."

At the query, Cannelli's eyes narrowed warily, but a second later he answered casually, "Hell, I guess you know as many places as I do, Tiger. I would like to meet your friend, though. At least I can pass the word to the bartender to use the good whisky..."

With this exchange, the club operator had quietly ushered Olsen out into the main room of the place. The band, accompanying a chorus number of all the "girls," brayed loudly. The customers seemed equally as boisterous, possibly anticipating the approaching closing hour. With a friendly clap on the back, Cannelli sent Tiger on the way back to his table, remarking that he would probably see him later.

On reaching the table that he had staggered from only a few minutes before, Tiger found that two other men, both obviously what they were, had joined Francis.

"Well, dearie, what were you doing so long in there—or what was doing you?" demanded Francis gayly.

"Believe it or not," Tiger grinned, "I met an old friend, and had a drink with him." He looked questioningly at the newcomers.

With a wave of his hand, Francis said, "Oh, just two more of the local girls. And this is my own Tiger," he added drunkenly for the strangers' benefit.

Tiger shook two moist, limp hands in succession, and was just seated, when one of them put a hand on his arm.

"Say, aren't you Tiger Olsen from the Marines?"

Tiger rather curtly acknowledged this, and shook off the hand. The gay one smirked and said loudly, "Why! I remember when you came back! I saw the parade and everything! And I've got all sorts of cute pictures of you in your football suit. Too bad you weren't a track man. They photograph so much more interestingly. Anyway, I've got all these pictures of you in my scrapbook of dream men. You just must come up to my place and see it."

Though carrying on a drunken conversation with the other stranger, Francis missed none of this, and was very amused at Tiger's flushed confusion. Fortunately, at this moment, Joe Cannelli came up to the table with a waiter bearing a round of drinks. He greeted Tiger again, and looked questioningly at the three seated with him.

"Just wanted to be sure that you got a round on the house, Tiger. We've got to treat these visitors from the East right."

At this, Tiger, hoping that the brevity of his introductions would be acceptable, said as casually as he could, "Francis, Joe Cannelli. He runs this place."

Francis rose and struck a more or less feminine pose. Shaking hands briefly, he quipped, "At least, Mr. Cannelli, I brought a man into the house." Joe laughed at this and admitted that not too many did come there. Turning again to Olsen, he spoke in a lowered voice, "When you leave here, your friend might like the Gourmand." At Tiger's puzzled look, he added, "It's an all night spot with plenty of all kinds of kicks. Tell 'em I sent you."

Tiger nodded his thanks as the club operator walked away. One of the characters at the table said, "My, Tiger! You do know the most exciting people."

Tiger ignored him and leaned closer over the table so that Francis could hear him over the bedlam of the club.

"Joe runs this joint, and I explained that you were a stranger in town and looking for anything for a thrill. I guess he had to size you up first. He must figure we're okay, because he suggested we try the Gourmand, wherever that is."

Francis grinned and nodded his approbation. More loudly, he replied, "Let's find out."

Turning to one of the habitues, he asked, "What kind of a spot is the Gourmand, dear?"

The one addressed rolled his eyes and gasped, "Oh, Bessie! That's one of those all night places, open from midnight to six in the morning."

"Do they serve drinks that late?" put in Olsen.

"Gawd yes!" gayly informed the other man. "At a price! You can get anything in that joint from a piece of trade to a main line shot—if you've got the money."

His companion seemed to take a dimmer view, and interrupted to say, "Well, I don't think it's safe there. They drink all night, and smoke weed, and turn tricks all over the place. I tell you, May, it's just too damned gay! They're due to be raided any time."

By this time Francis had gotten the idea, and noticing that the crowd in the Bait Room was thinning out, he finished his drink, much of which he had already slopped under the table unnoticed.

"Let's all go there, then," he giggled. "The night's still real young."

The strange pair looked at each other, and Francis hastily added, "Oh, come on, you two. The party's on me!"

"Oh dear, I'd love to, but my husband is around here somewhere. I'd better find him."

As if on cue, another nervous character swished up to the group at the table, and began upbraiding the speaker. This turned out to be the "husband." As soon as the invitation had been made clear to him, he too, with an interested survey of Tiger, was ready to go. And so, rising, with many girlish and attention-getting cries of pleasure and wit, the party finally made its way out of the Bait Room.

Outside, many taxis were taking off the crowd that was now surging from the place. Tiger mentioned that he had his car, but that it would only hold two. Francis, who was obviously expected to finance the trip, waved at a cab, and sent Tiger off to the parking lot with the admirer who kept a scrapbook.

Some twenty minutes or so later, Tiger pulled up to the curb before a dingy building on a dark street, in what was almost a slum section. Francis and his two companions were waiting at the door to the place. Tiger was now alone, and at Francis' amused query, he explained: "That's just a great big mixed-up kid. He got awfully sleepy all of a sudden and had to go home."

Francis, noting that Tiger massaged a slightly reddened knuckle, laughed, and said, "Oh, you rough thing!" as they turned to the dim doorway of the Gourmand Club.

Chapter Thirteen

Leaving his office after some final discussion with Captain Morphy and the government agent, Captain Starr turned in at Flanagan's for a nightcap. He rather pleasantly anticipated the peace and quiet of the Back Room. He was a little surprised to find Senator Martin there. The senator greeted him casually, saying something about a phone call.

The socialite, who never had been particularly friendly with the police officer, had obviously been at some dressy function; also, he suddenly seemed unusually affable.

As there were only the two gentlemen present, after the waiter had brought drinks, it was not unusual that Martin should comment on the newest features of the three murders, which were emblazoned in the headlines of all the late editions.

"My, Captain," said the Senator, "you do seem to have problems these days. Or, are these Captain Morphy's...?"

While the officer unconsciously glanced around to make sure that they were alone, he certainly had no hesitation in discussing the case with such a prominent and discreet citizen as Senator Martin.

"No, these are mine. Though because of the police characters involved, Morphy's as well as other outfits, all have an interest."

"That's interesting, Starr. Though from all I could see with only a glance at the headlines, this is just a series of killings."

The police officer sighed. "I wish it were that simple, but there seems to be vice, bunco, blackmail, and other things besides homicide."

The elderly man grimaced expressively.

"That really seems to be a complete calendar of misdeeds. 'Other things'—humph!" he mused as if half to himself. Then he smiled as he remarked with the merest suggestion of sarcasm, "I suppose that actually these 'other things' include driving in the wrong lane, or overtime parking?"

Whether Senator Martin's acid comment was intended to irritate him or not escaped Captain Starr at the moment as he rather heatedly replied, "As a matter of fact, Senator, the 'other things' involve a very widespread distribution of narcotics."

"Oh," said Martin, registering proper appreciation, "but I suppose that all you people will have it run down within a day or so."

Captain Starr was tired, and in consequence only gave his answer a slight consideration. "I hope so! We do have several leads. Say, Senator! You know a lot of people. Are you acquainted with a brother and sister by the name of Holden? They do live out your way. I believe that their parents both died some years ago. And I think that these people own considerable property."

After a moment's consideration, the older man nodded. "Yes, I think that I've met an Arthur Holden, and I believe that he does have a sister. And their parents were killed, too. But how in the world do they fit into this thing?"

"Well, it's this third man that was killed; though he was actually killed first. Oh, it's all pretty confused. But anyway, his sister mentioned this evening that her brother kept a diary, and when we get hold of it tomorrow, we just may find something in it that will lead us to whoever murdered these three men."

"I see," said the Senator, "but why, if this is such an important lead, are you waiting for tomorrow?"

Captain Starr grinned involuntarily at Martin's stiff manner.

"You see, sir, his sister hasn't been told as yet that Arthur Holden is dead. So when we sent her home to get the diary she thought only that he was 'missing.' Part of our plan at that time was to delay telling her or publicly identifying the victim. But somehow it seems to have leaked to the papers. So we'll wait until tomorrow to pick up the diary, if there really is one."

"Hmmm! Yes, I suppose that I do see it. All very complicated, isn't it? Well, Captain, it doesn't look like my party will call, so perhaps I'd better be getting along. Best of luck in running down your man."

With a sudden partial return to his customary caution, Captain Starr realized that he had said much more than he had intended. Of course, anything was all right with the Senator, still—"Uh, Senator, I'd appreciate it if what I've said went no farther for the time being."

Adjusting his homburg and smiling jovially, Martin clasped Starr's hand briefly, as was not unusual at the parting of two friends with a single purpose.

"But of course, Captain," he assured. "And I must really be getting along. Goodnight! I shall see you soon, perhaps."

"Goodnight, sir," respectfully replied the tired Captain, who was really wondering whether he should have another drink or get up and go home also.

The eye inspecting the party through the hole in the door of the Gourmand Club was cold and disinterested until Tiger mentioned that Joe Cannelli had sent them. At this, and much to their surprise, the group was welcomed and ushered in with most abject apologies for the delay.

Their greeter's manner was now effusive as they passed down a narrow, poorly lighted hallway. One of Francis' guests—the pair had expressed a desire to be called Frankie and Johnnie, though it was not clear in Tiger's mind which was which—laughingly remarked of their guide, "Get her, she's tee'd to the ears."

The party was led into a room which, because of its darkness, at first defied description. On becoming more accustomed to the light provided by a single enormous candle set in some sort of holder in the middle of the room and the few other small candles winking in the fringing darkness, they could dimly make out a surrounding ring of upholstered booths. Some of these had curtains drawn before them, but those that were open appeared to be filled with people who were drinking and laughing and obviously enjoying themselves in a normal cocktail-lounge fashion. An unseen pianist somewhere in the murky background was playing boogie and bebop on an instrument that sounded bizarrely out of tune. Of course, it could have been the player.

Their guide installed them in a booth, and when they were seated he asked what they would have.

There was, Tiger noted, a slightly dazed expression on this character's face. He seemed to speak jerkily as if his sense of timing were not functioning. But Olsen did not pay too much attention, being momentarily arrested by the sight revealed across the room as a curtain billowed away from before a booth on a sudden current of air. What took Tiger's eye was not an illusion. Two servicemen, and in uniform, were wrapped together in a desperately passionate embrace. These two, locked together lip to lip and hip to hip, were completely oblivious of all around them.

Olsen nudged Francis. "Hey, get a load of that action."

Not only Francis stared at the straining couple, but Frankie and Johnnie and the waiter did also.

"Well!" exclaimed Francis emphatically, "The birds and the bees. Don't those two ever come up for air?"

The house character laughed shrilly at this. "Get you, May! Ya shoulda seen those two an hour ago when they got started. Hell! Now that they are back up on their feet and buttoned up, they're just saying goodnight."

Tiger shook his head, and muttered, "Helluva long goodnight."

"Oh," smirked the waiter, "they been blasting, two or three sticks a piece, and now they've got nothing but time. Say," he said, suddenly recalling that business came first, "you girls didn't bring a bottle, so what d'ya want?"

As Tiger hesitated, and Frankie end Johnnie were guests anyway, Francis spoke up. "Well, dearie, Cannelli said we could really have us a gay time here, so better make it the works."

"Yeah," naively put in Tiger, "let's have some drinks."

"Okay," said the waiter, and as Frankie and Johnnie nodded, he added, "'spose I might as well save a trip. What else d'ya need?"

Noting a hesitation, he laughed and added gayly, "Come on, girls! Let's live it up! A few sticks, maybe—or do ya want a fix?"

One of his "guests" turned eagerly to Francis: "Let's blast a few, dear. Okay?"

Francis nodded in agreement, as if just getting the idea.

"Make it the works, Kate. A bottle of Scotch, and about a dozen sticks. We'll see where that gets us."

The waiter laughed shrilly, and flounced off into the flickering shadows.

Tiger looked around the now more discernable room and saw that there was another ring of booths behind the one in which they were seated. These outer and larger booths were also filled, some with larger parties. The people he could see were of all races and colors, and were more or less similar to the brassy crowd in the Bait Room.

There were only one or two women present, Tiger realized quickly, as his eye fell on one who sat back in the corner of one of those distant compartments. From the distance, the details were not too clear. And if it had not been for the fact that all that was visible of the girl—above the table, anyway—was completely nude, he might not even have noticed her.

Lounging beside her was a burly masculine type, who was sprawled partially across the table, one hand tentatively fondling the really large breasts of his companion.

Olsen was very naturally interested and continued to watch as this person removed his glasses, which he placed carefully on the table. Then he put his cigar in an ashtray; and letting his fingers trail over and down and under the protruding flesh, he was suddenly lost to view as he buried his head in the girl's lap.

The lady smoked on unconcernedly, staring with complete indifference into nothingness. Only a slightly rhythmic jerking of her outstanding breasts indicated that she was alive.

"Get that fish queen!" simpered Johnnie, in patent disgust.

His friend smirkingly agreed with him: "Gawd, yes! Things like that give us honest girls a bad name."

At this point the waiter returned and unceremoniously dumped a bottle on the table. This was labeled "Scotch Whisky"; and in consideration of the fact that the party had been sent by Joe Cannelli, it probably had a considerable percentage of that delightful beverage in it. Also plopped down were a bowl of ice, some glasses, and a short stubby section of candle similar to those they had noticed in other booths. Fishing in a pocket, the waiter brought out an apparently ordinary though opened pack of cigarettes of a popular brand. This last item he did not quite let out of his hands, as he blithely said, "That'll be thirty dollars, dearie..."

Tiger started to explode in indignation, but Francis stepped on his toe and gripped his arm as he got out his wallet. Counting out the money, he laughingly thanked the waiter, and suggested that he return later.

At a nod from Francis, the two friends reached for the cigarettes. They quickly removed a couple of ordinary smokes from the pack, throwing them down on the table. As one lit the stub of candle, the other took out of the pack two smaller hand-rolled cigarettes. These were slightly shorter than the pack's usual content. Tiger noticed that the ends of these cigarettes had been carefully tucked in so as to preserve every shred of the "tobacco."

Francis warily watched this procedure while quickly pouring and downing several drinks from the bottle. As the two gleefully lit each other's cigarettes, Francis whispered to Tiger, "Take it easy with that weed. We've got work to do."

By now Frankie and Johnnie had taken long deep drags on their smokes, and were happily holding the fumes as deeply as possible in their lungs. As one exhaled, reluctantly, the smoke was accompanied by a little giggle. This caused the other to laugh aloud—and this set the pattern for the next hour.

As Francis very obviously did not care to indulge, he had excused himself, indicating the whisky and saying gayly, "I'd love to, girls. But you know, they really don't mix."

After a time, the waiter passed by and stopped to chat with Francis.

Tiger felt a bit out of it all, so he casually picked up one of the smokes the pair next to him found so enjoyable. Preparing it as they had, he soon had it alight and inhaled deeply. At the expression on his face, as the bitter acrid smoke bit into his throat and lungs, Frankie and Johnnie shrieked in merry amusement. Francis frowned.

This last was noticed by the observant waiter, who laughingly remarked, "Start 'em young, I always say! Anyway, dearie, he'll be just too weak to resist after a couple of those."

Francis laughed, but Tiger, who had overheard the remark and understood its meaning, leaned forward belligerently, growling, "Listen, Buster…"

At this the houseman again laughed, though he edged away from the table and out of reach. "Get you, doll!" he teased. "Buster isn't here tonight. Probably over at the Baths. But I'm sure that you and he should meet."

Noting Francis' interested expression, which had been alerted at the mention of the "baths," the waiter explained: "Buster is our troubleshooter and part-time bouncer, though he does seem to work more at the baths, lately. Anyway, he's about this one's size and type. I'll bet they'd do it real pretty."

Here Johnnie broke into the conversation. "You can have that one, dearie. He plays too damned rough! Did you hear about that belle he beat up—and knocked out one of her eyes?"

"Yes," agreed the waiter, helping himself to a drink, "but that's the way it goes, girl. We all get our kicks in different ways. Buster is really a nice guy. But I'll admit, he does play rough."

Frankie blurted out, "You'll never convince me that Buster didn't have something to do with that Kay! Why, they were shacked up together."

The waiter leaned over the table ominously, and catching Frankie's arm, said, "Listen, doll, we don't talk about Kay around here." Turning to Francis and Tiger, he gayly explained, "Some snotty young queen who used to hang around here shot herself with another guy. They were lovers, I guess." Shrugging his shoulders and downing another drink—and with a final glare at Frankie and Johnnie—the waiter swished away from the table.

Tiger, more or less incoherently, started to ask something of Francis, but his query dwindled off into nothingness. Through it, however, Francis just barely over-heard Frankie mutter, evidently speaking of the waiter, "Get that one! Took over Kay's job, maybe Buster, too."

And, to this Johnnie replied, "Yeah, don't think I'd like to be in her shoes."

It was almost an hour later. Frankie and Johnnie had found an acquaintance, a type called "Polly," and he had joined the party. All three were busy with their smokes, tittering and laughing merrily and inanely. Francis had been listening for any further reference to Kay, and had been steadily pouring drinks for himself. When unobserved, he'd pour these drinks on the floor under the table.

When Tiger had picked up a second of the hand-made cigarettes, Francis had firmly taken it out of his hand. The big ex-athlete seemed happily acquiescent, though he had also begun to giggle slightly. Francis realized that it was time to make another move.

"My God," he gasped, fanning the air about him, "it's too damned hot in here."

The marijuana smokers laughed hilariously at this, and the newest addition said, "Well, dear, let's go somewhere else."

This was just the opening that Francis had been waiting for.

"Okay, girls. But where'll we go at this time of the night? Remember, I'm a stranger in town."

Frankie said, "Let's go down to the Square and get some trade."

Polly promptly vetoed this suggestion. "Oh, you and your hustling trade! They're all shopworn anyway."

Johnnie, suddenly inspired, cried, "Girls! I know! Let's go to the Baths."

The late arrival, being more practical or possibly less high, asked, "That's an idea, but can we afford it?"

Johnnie volunteered, "Oh, it's not so expensive, if you don't go in for those fancy deals upstairs."

Francis stood up and, motioning to the now empty bottle and to Tiger who was resting easily with his head on the table, said, "Come on, kids. I've got some money left. Besides, you'll have to help me with this one. It looks like I'm going to have to steam him up a bit."

With the three friends laughing merrily as they assisted Tiger to his feet, Francis realized that his big assistant was quite drunk. He hoped, however, that a lot of this was for the benefit of the others. Outside the Gourmand, the cold fog-laden air cleared Francis' head. It didn't seem to affect the others, who chatted gayly as they waited to flag down a passing cab. Finally a cab appeared and they all crowded into it, with Tiger safely between Francis and the driver.

"Where to, Mac?" asked the hacker.

"Let me see," said Francis, turning to the three in the rear, who merrily supplied the address. "But wait a minute," Francis added as the driver started to get under way. "You've got a radio, call the dispatcher and have him send out an extra driver, someone who can handle a Jaguar."

He indicated the small sports car at the near curb.

Within a very few minutes, another cab pulled up, and an extra man was given the keys, which Francis had taken from Tiger's pocket. The cab drivers carefully compared the car registration with Olsen's identifications, and agreed to take the sports car into the company garage until he should call for it. This, it seemed, was a customary service.

When this transaction was all completed, Francis leaned tiredly back in the small part of the seat that the apparently sleeping Olsen left unoccupied.

"Okay," he caroled gayly, "off to the baths, girls. Come who may..."

Chapter Fourteen

The Baths were situated in an old but respectable looking building in the more commercial part of a section of the city that had been rezoned for what was locally called "the trade." The building had actually come into existence some years before as the handsome annex to a school for young misses—since destroyed, the school, that is.

On the demise of this academy and up to the more recent cutting of a freeway—a deep roofless tunnel—through the property and just to the rear of the building, the structure was variously used and abused until finally it had inconspicuously put forth a small and tasteful neon sign—"BATHS."

A vacant lot at one side afforded ample parking space, aside from the usually deserted night curbs. The neighborhood was more or less central in the city, and the usual quiet was only disturbed by the swish and hum of the fast traffic in the deep cut along the rear of the building. While the "bathhouse" was an ample three stories in height, the rear windows were actually again as high above the busy motor concourse below. Aside from the discreet lights of the small foyer at the entrance, all windows in the building had been carefully covered, and from three sides the old structure sat mute and dark.

After paying off the taxi and unloading the complacently agreeable Olsen, Francis stopped his little party at the entrance to the baths. "Just what is the setup in here, dear?" he asked of Polly.

"Well, it's three dollars each, to get in," said that one, characteristically happy to be an authority on something, "and you check your jewels and wallet and stuff at the desk." Here Polly leered. "And, of course, if you want any of the 'special features' you'd better carry a few dollars in with you. But do check your jewels—watch and ring and stuff like that. Then you register, just like for a hotel. They give you a skimpy towel or two and you go on back to those little rooms. Of course, all the girls call 'em cribs! Then you put all your clothes in the locker in your room and then you drape a towel around your hips and come out and cruise."

"Where's the 'bath' come in?" demanded the Tiger, suddenly alive.

"Oh you! You'll never get to it! There are a couple of showers at the back, and a sort of steam room and toilets and stuff. But most everyone just cruises around. If you see an open door, and someone interesting is inside, you go on in."

The large ex-Marine yawned and muttered, "Yeah. Well I just want to crap out in the sack for a couple of hours."

Johnnie said, "You'd better close your door tight, then, handsome; or you're due for a helluva lot of company."

Tiger looked around and, glancing at Francis who blushed becomingly, slyly winked and said, "I've already got a lot of company."

Feeling that this line was getting nowhere, Francis hurriedly asked, "What's this about 'special features'?"

"Oh," said the verbose Polly, "that's mostly for the rich old aunties, and bats like that. You have to go upstairs. They have some special 'masseurs' up there—at stud! Then, they have shows and exhibitions; but it runs into money. I've never been up, but a queen I know told me that they've had some trouble up there lately."

"That's where that Kay used to work, or she said she did, anyway. Besides, that Buster—he lives up there, I think." offered Frankie.

"That one!" exclaimed Johnnie. "He's too rough for me. He beat up a girl at the Gourmand one night when he was high, and they had to take her to the hospital. He's crazy when he's loaded."

"Did you get that waiter back there? She got all excited when we mentioned Kay. I guess that's Buster's new friend. But she can have my share," added Polly. To Francis he continued, "Anyway, dear, you shouldn't worry about going upstairs. You've got all you need right with you." This last was accompanied by a leer in Tiger's direction.

Francis was a little worried by these tentative overtures, not having any idea as to how the so-far patient Olsen might react. He quickly led the group inside.

A short while later, and after the party had been 'processed', they once again got together in one of the narrow hallways that ran between the tiny rooms. Each was clothed now only in a narrow towel, draped jauntily or otherwise around the middle. The only other item of apparel was the key on a heavy rubber band. The three who had been there before wore this around the upper arm like a bracelet. Fingering his own before he slipped it onto his arm, Francis was soberly reminded of a similar key he had examined some hours before in the morgue.

There was considerable "traffic" cruising past the group with much obvious interest. Most of these were middle-aged and elderly men, all of whom stared unabashedly at the well-fleshed and muscular bodies of Tiger and Francis. A few exchanged greetings with Polly, Frankie, and Johnnie. And these three in due course drifted away on pursuits of their own. Francis and Tiger lounged tiredly in a doorway, and for a few minutes quietly compared notes.

"Well, muscles, it's been a long day, hasn't it?" grinned Francis.

"F'god sakes, boss!" groaned Tiger, who was actually not as knocked-out as he appeared to be, "You said the work would be different. But how different can it get?"

"Okay, fella. Keep your chin up."

"That's about all I could get up this morning," cracked Olsen.

Looking down the passageway behind Tiger, Francis noted an elderly "bather" who had prowled past them several times. He was now talking with a very tall, skinny man dressed in whites. Obviously an attendant. As Francis or Tiger seemed to be the subject of the conversation, Francis was not too surprised when they were presently approached by the man in white.

"Hello, you two," he greeted them with the same girlish effusiveness that seemed characteristic of all the people they'd met during the night. "Are you having fun?"

Tiger grinned and leered drunkenly, and Francis quickly said, "Dearie, we've had it. Do you run this place?"

"Well, I'm sort of the Madame, Stepladder Kate, the boys all call me." Looking about cautiously, he came closer and in a lowered voice continued, "Would you two like to make a little money this morning?"

"Doing what?" cautiously asked Francis.

"Well, dearie, you see, it's like this. I know that you two are new here. And that's what we like to see—fresh faces," he said with a glance at Tiger's draped mid-section. "Polly says that you're okay, and so do the others—"

"Come on, girl. Get with it," prompted Francis.

"Oh, okay! You see, we've got a lot of customers that like to see exhibitions. You know what I mean."

Tiger looked a bit bewildered, but Francis nodded that he understood. The "Madame" continued, "Now you two are a real pretty couple. Yes," he enthused, looking them over closely, "real pretty!"

Francis noticed one of Tiger's fists clenching, and he quickly intervened to demand a cigarette and a light, which the character supplied as Francis remarked, "All right, dearie. And we're on our honeymoon, so what's with it?"

"Well, we have a room upstairs, and it's really very nicely furnished. There's a big comfortable bed and—well, it's real nice, see. Then there are rooms on both sides, and people can look into the middle room without being seen. So, we put on some real gay parties for them to watch, and stuff like that."

"Yeah, sounds real cozy," offered Francis, "but where do we come in?"

"Oh, that. There's an old bat who would like to watch you and this one play. So if you'd like to make a few bucks, and enjoy yourself comfortably while doing it—"

"Aaah!" Tiger said disgustedly.

"No," said Francis. "I'm not sure that we have any play

left this morning. Some other time, maybe."

Noticing that Tiger's attention was momentarily on two men down the passageway who had removed their towels and were appraising each other's charms, Stepladder Kate motioned Francis a few feet to one side.

"Listen, do you think that your friend would just pose, alone and stripped, like the ones they have in those muscle magazines? Real harmless stuff."

"Alone? All by himself?" asked Francis, wondering if this was a lead to what they sought.

"This old guy's real hot, and he's got plenty of loot!" said Kate.

"What kind of pictures?"

"Oh, just the usual 'art poses' like they sell, like the ones in the books."

"Alone?" asked Francis, while quickly turning over in his mind the advisibility of going further with this.

"Why certainly! There'd be nobody except Buster in the studio with him. Buster's the photographer."

The name alerted Francis at once, though he maintained a show of disinterest. "No playing around?"

"For God's sake, Bessie! Are you afraid someone'll steal his cherry? Of course he'll be alone, except for Buster—and the pictures."

"Hey, what do you mean, 'Buster and the pictures'?"

Kate laughed shrilly. "Oh! That's part of the gag, dearie! Y'see, we get a lot of reluctant fellows who are real pretty, like this one; but finally, for a few dollars, they will pose alone. So, Buster gets 'em up on the model stand, and while he 'adjusts' the camera some sidelights go on that light up some big 'action pictures' that are right in front of the model. Well! These are some shots of some of the parties we have had up there. And believe me, my dear, they are real active! You can imagine what looking at them for a few minutes will do to the bashful model. Everything is soon standing on its own, and that's when Buster takes the pictures. Some of these old guys will pay real good for prints of that kind. Listen, Bess, if you can get handsome there to pose, I'll get Buster to save you some copies for your scrapbook."

"Yeah, I see what you mean," said Francis, whose mind was busily considering all the possibilities. "Well, I'm tired. But maybe I can talk him into it. One thing: he's new at all this, so nobody had better get too close or bother him, because I think he'd get real rough. Okay?"

"Oh you! Certainly it'll be okay! Did you say that you were new here in Bay City?"

"Why, yes. But I've got a lot of friends."

"You must have, May! They called and okayed you from the Gourmand—said that you were friends of Joe…"

"Joe?"

"Sure, girl. Joe Cannelli—"

"Oh, that one! Well, as a matter of fact, they're all friends of Tiger. That's the lug with me."

"I see. He sorta reminds me of someone, but I just can't remember who. Oh, well! Wishful thinking, I guess."

Francis turned back toward his assistant, "I'll see what I can do about that, but—" He shook his head doubtfully, indicating the big, stripped ex-marine.

"Okay," said Kate. "I'll be in front here by the stairs."

Francis joined Tiger who was grinningly engrossed with the two men farther down the passageway. Both were now handling the merchandise, with some interest. The "merchandise," however, showed no interest at all. But it was still early in the morning. Francis nudged the head-shaking Olsen into a room and closed the door.

"I'm a son of a bitch!" exclaimed the ex-athlete. "I thought I saw everything in the Marine Corps. But if anybody had told me there were joints like this in my own home town—Hey, boss, let's clean house."

"Uh-uh, Tiger. Now listen to me a minute. I think I've got all that we came for, information anyway. But, I'd like to know about those private rooms upstairs."

He quickly explained all that had been told him by the houseman, and the offer that had come with it.

"Now, look, Tiger, I can't cold-bloodedly ask you to do this. But I do wish that you could see that it would sure help us. If you would only agree to pose, and then get up there and just stall. I don't think it would be a good idea to let this gang get any pictures of you stripped, though a nice big enlargement would make a dandy ornament on the wall over Hattie's desk. But, kidding aside, I'd like to get up there, and this might be our chance. As I see it now, these pictures could be at the bottom of the blackmail racket, but I'm not sure. You could size up the layout, and after you go up I'll try to follow you. Maybe we could both get a look around. So, what do you say?"

"Oh, shit!" said the tired Tiger. "Anything for dear old alma agency. But if some bastard gets too busy, I'm gonna slug him."

"Sure, sure, Tiger, But try to keep it down. Remember, we gotta get out of here, and with our clothes and stuff in the office, too. This ought not to take more than half an hour, and then we can go home and get some sleep. Boy, I'm pooped!" yawned Francis.

Tiger grinned. "Yeah! You're pooped. Get me!"

He turned and, hitching his towel more securely about his lean hips, left the cubicle and headed for the stairs.

Chapter Fifteen

The Baths manager led Tiger up the stairs to the next floor. Stairs, Tiger noted, also continued up to the third story; and a side stairway descended as well. As nearly as Olsen could recall the outside aspects of the building, these probably led to the parking lot side, where there was probably another entrance.

With a continuous "gay" conversation, Kate ushered Tiger into a fairly large room, whose only discernible furniture was a great, low bed. This was opulently covered with some dark fur-like material, and was handily furnished with half a dozen gayly colored pillows and cushions. As Tiger looked about him, the "Madame" said, "It's a gorgeous workbench, isn't it? Like something out of DeMille! And if it could talk! The mad affairs that have taken place on that couch..."

Olsen continued to look about the exotic room as this prattle continued. To one side and in a corner was a small raised platform with a classic-styled broken pillar on it. Across the room, and so situated that it was in easy range of either the bed or the model stand, was a large and complicated camera on a tripod. This was only partly hidden by a heavy, movable, folding screen.

On close inspection, Tiger noted that a wide frieze ran around the room just at eye-level. Stepping nearer, this was revealed as a series of enlarged "action pictures" of men and women in various indescribable poses and positions. Even the detail, seen at a glance, brought a blush to Tiger's countenance. Obviously most of the pictures had been taken in this room on and about the great "workbench." It was also apparent that this band of art studies could be lighted up when needed to inspire other models.

Short curtains were drawn across wide spaces in each side wall. One, slightly parted, revealed a mirror beneath. With only a glance at this unusual arrangement, Tiger was aware that his guide was still talking.

"...and so if you'll just wait here for a few minutes— Buster has probably gone upstairs. I think I heard his phone ring..."

"Who's Buster?" growled the tired Tiger.

"Oh, Buster's the photographer," Kate explained, and, suddenly aware of Olsen's obvious truculence, added, "He's also the bouncer. That is, he takes care of any trouble we might have in the house."

The veiled but implied threat of this last brought a grin to Tiger's face. "Well, okay, dearie. Unleash the dogs."

Nose in the air, Stepladder Kate flounced out. The door closed behind him with a decided click. Tiger at once tried it and found that he was locked in.

Broadminded Tiger had up to this point been more or less amused by the events of the whole mad evening. The locked door, however, made him very definitely unhappy. Feeling the panel over, he at once realized that it was either metal or well reinforced. At this moment it was a very angry ex-captain of Marines who stood in the center of the "party room," weighing possibilities.

Swift thoughts of demolishment and mayhem were as quickly dispelled as the door opened and an elderly and distinguished looking gentleman entered. Before he could close the open door behind him, Tiger pushed him rudely aside, and propped the portal completely open with the corner of a heavy screen. Turning to his visitor, Tiger angrily demanded, "Are you Buster?"

"Heavens no!" was the amused reply. "Buster is more your size and type. Say! I know you! You're Tiger Olsen."

"Yeah? So what?"

"Why, er, nothing, except that I remember you well. My! What are you doing here?"

"Listen, Mister! I'm just a tourist, see! Not that it's anybody's goddamned business what I'm doing here. So, somebody wanted to take some pictures of my friend, but he doesn't feel so good. And I offered to pose. And all by myself, too! Now, what goes on here? And how come that door got locked?"

This all came out explosively as Tiger, fists clenched at his sides, stood belligerently over the older man, who now lolled back across the bed.

"Oh, come on, Olsen, simmer down. Nobody's going to hurt you. I saw that you were annoyed when Kate went out and locked you in, so I came over before you could wreck the joint."

Tiger was forced to smile at the disarming tone, as well as at the probable truth of the man's surmise.

"How do you mean—you 'saw' me?"

The man rose and walked to one of the draped side walls. There he pulled back the curtains to either side, revealing a simple, large, plate glass mirror. Turning to the puzzled Olsen, he explained, "These are really tricky. They are mirrors on this side, but you can see through them just as if they were windows from the other side. That's why they have them here on both sides of the 'party room.' The spectators are in the rooms at either side. Then, too, this whole place is wired for sound. I heard Kate say that she was going to get Buster."

"Well, I'll be damned!" said Olsen. "Look, I'm sorry if I got sore. I guess I'm just tired. We've had a helluva night; and then some old bastard wanted us to pose for some pictures—" Tiger stopped, flushing with a sudden perception.

"Yeah, Tiger. I'm the old bastard. I guess I'm too old to play games anymore, but I do get a bang out of watching. Besides, I have an amazing collection of pictures. I certainly never thought I'd get one of Tiger Olsen. If Bruce hears about this, he'll raise the prices."

"Well, if that picture snapper don't get here pretty quick, I'm going home. Say, you don't seem like such—well, I mean, that is—you're not silly like those assholes downstairs."

"Thanks, Tiger. And you don't seem so wise yet that you should be in a place like this. As a matter of fact, if you'll take a tip from me, you'll get the hell out of here and stay away. I know that I'm here a lot, but there are some pretty rotten things in this setup." The gentleman stopped talking as Francis appeared in the doorway.

"Well, Tiger! Where did you get to? Need any help?" asked Francis, not quite sure of the situation.

"No. Everything's okay here, except that I'm supposed to be waiting for that tall guy."

At this, the "Madame" appeared behind Francis, apparently very nervous or excited about something. His voice was unusually shrill.

"Ladies! What goes on here—a daisy chain? Buster was called away very urgently, and I must close off these upper floors. So, we'll just have to forget our little arrangement, and get our pictures some other time."

With a running-fire of this sort of chatter, he quickly ushered the three men downstairs, where the distinguished old man lingeringly clasped Tiger's hand in parting.

Tiger and Francis thankfully went to their rooms to dress. Fifteen minutes later they were in a taxi, heading for home. It was 7:45 A.M.

Chapter Sixteen

Shortly after ten o'clock the same morning, Francis briskly entered the offices of the Morley Agency. He was greeted by a slightly acid Hattie.

"Banker's hours, eh, Mr. Morley?"

Francis stopped at his receptionist's desk and, after a slight pause during which he rapidly counted to ten, answered smilingly, "No, Hattie dear, not banker's hours. But, should you care, Bessie, Tiger and I were with the police on a triple murder the entire night. We got home at about eight, two hours ago. I for one had just time to change, clean up, have coffee and get down here—to be nagged as I come in the door. Now, if you think that is a sufficient résumé of my night, we can proceed. What's doing?"

"Oh, well, I'm sorry, Mr. Morley, but it's been quite a morning. Those decorators are in the spare, that is, Mr. Olsen's office, and there is some sort of hassle on about some 'off-pink' drapes."

"I'm sure he'll adore off-pink."

"Yes! I can see what you mean. Then there have been more applicants for the job. How is Mr. Olsen working out?"

"Just peachy! Frankly, dear, I only hired him because I could see that he was just your type. And I do so want to keep you happy."

"Oh, Mr. Morley..." The secretary blushed becomingly, and laughed.

"Miss Campbell, I'm just a trifle unwell this morning. Now, please, stop twittering. Has anything important come up?"

"I was just getting to this, sir!" snapped Hattie with considerable hauteur, "Captain Starr has called several times."

"Now that, toots, is more like it."

Francis turned to his own office. Just as he reached the door to his private domain, he heard Hattie offer: "If I felt that bad in the mornings, I'd do something about it."

Francis paused and turned patiently, realizing that his secretary was really only trying to be helpful in her own way. "And what, dearie, aside from Lydia Pinkhams or a whirling spray would you suggest?"

Hattie, mollified by Francis' seemingly receptive attitude, said brightly, "Mr. Morley, have you ever tried one of those Turkish Baths?"

Francis stared at the woman in sheer amazement; then, mouthing a horrible moan, he fled into his own sanctuary, slamming the door behind him.

Hattie, at her desk, upright and slightly offended, spoke only to the wall calendar when she muttered, "Get her!"

After a quick Bromo, neatly chased by a large slug of Metaxa, a bottle of which he had thoughtfully laid in the day before for just such emergencies, Francis felt revived. He had barely got this potion down, and was considering writing a concise report of the night's activities, when the door burst open and in walked Captain Starr.

"Good morning, Captain—or is it? Take that chair over there."

After returning the greeting gruffly and seating himself, the homicide officer came abruptly to the point of his visit.

"Morley, I'm afraid that we all got a little carried away last night. That is, this seems to be a routine police matter. And after some consideration I don't think that the Department would care to be in the position of turning this thing over to a private agency."

Francis interrupted. "I can see your point, Captain Starr, but I thought that we were all agreed that speed was of the essence, er, really vital in this, and that acting unofficially I might be able to do what the known police could not."

"Well, yes. We did say that. But—"

Francis slid some loose papers across the desk.

"Perhaps you'd like to make some notes, Captain."

"What d'ya mean?"

"First, the narcotics." Francis leaned back in his chair, and then with a sudden inspiration he leaned forward and flicked a key. "Miss Campbell. Please put this on tape and transcribe it later, two copies. This is a summation of a report entailing conversation between myself and my assistant, Mr. Olsen. Do you understand, Hattie? There are just Olsen and myself present."

"I understand, Mr. Morley. This conversation of an agency report is informal and between you and Mr. Olsen. Okay, I've got it. Good morning, Captain."

Captain Starr started to respond to the greeting, but at a motion from Francis growled unintelligibly instead. Then he demanded, "What's all this monkey business about?"

Francis switched the intercom off momentarily and replied, "I just thought that I could make a report for my files and possibly a copy for you as well. By using Olsen's name, Captain, we can keep anything official out of it. Now," he again switched the key to "ON": "The narcotics angle," Francis began.

"Yeah!" muttered Captain Starr skeptically.

"My assistant and I went to the Bait Room and there met personally a Mr. Joe Cannelli, the operator of that place."

"No!" exclaimed the police officer.

"We asked where something more lively might be obtained, and he—Cannelli—sent us to a place called the Gourmand, also owned and operated by Cannelli. By now there were four in the party, all of whom will be available as witnesses. We were admitted at the Gourmand only because Cannelli had phoned and okayed us. This was just after 2:00 A.M., but we were offered and served whisky. About a hundred other patrons were similarly served— until about 4:30 A.M., when we left. We were offered and sold marijuana. At least two of my party used these cigarettes there. Others about the place were openly using this narcotic, which was openly supplied by the waiter. The same waiter also offered a 'fix,' or a short supply of cocaine. Other drugs were suggested as available. Cannelli seems to have an overall control on this distribution. But between he and the passer—that is, the waiter who made the actual sale—there is another character, whom we didn't see, named Buster."

Francis paused for breath, then continued: "Another spot, where we were also okayed by Cannelli, was the "Baths." This would seem to tie up at least three joints with Mr. Cannelli, with dope sales in at least one and 'steerers' in the others. There are four witnesses to all of this activity. Now, does that tie up the narcotics angle?"

Open-mouthed, the police officer stared at Francis. Finally he shook his head as if in complete disbelief, and only remarked: "I'm a son of a bitch!"

Francis nodded as if incomplete agreement, and cheerily went on: "Next, we have a blackmail pattern that seems to lead to these deviate murders. We have located and personally inspected one setup around which all of this could and may revolve. We found steerers in three or four deviate hangouts, all steering to the 'Baths.' This is a sort of boarding house, self-service sex bargain counter for men only. That is, it's a place men go for men who go for men, if you follow me. I understand also that the establishment is only two short blocks from the Northern police station, but has been in uninterrupted operation for several years. The place has some very interesting sidelines. A complete photographic studio does pictures of various persons in various compromising positions. These pictures may or may not be taken with the subject's knowledge. There is every indication that this department of the Baths is frequented by many gentlemen of means. Now, here is an angle. The photographer is a guy named Buster, the same one that more or less manages the Gourmand. His late assistant was Kay Dunbar; and there is a definite rumor among the 'boys' that Kay got to know too much and Buster disposed of him. The man is—we heard many times—a muscular masochist and confines his pleasures to young and attractive men. We know that whoever killed Dunbar also murdered at least two others. It could have been this Buster, as far as our observations have told us; though we have not yet seen the man."

Francis clicked off the intercom and leaned back in his chair.

"Now, Captain," he said, "how's that for a night's work on your 'police matter'?"

The veteran officer shook his head. "I don't get it! A stranger in town, and, why we—"

Francis interrupted, "As I told you, I can get into these places." Leaning again over the desk set, Francis instructed Hattie to make up two copies of the report, and then to clear the tape. Turning to the homicide officer, he continued, "If I might make a suggestion, Captain, your Captain Morphy of the vice squad gave us the names of several places last night, all 'gay' joints. There were five of these baths mentioned. Now, as I see it, the bars and clubs all have something to sell, something from which an ostensible profit may be legitimately derived. The baths on the other hand can only bring in a return in rentals, as far as the owners of the properties are concerned. I would suggest that someone find out who owns these five places. Very possibly they may be acquaintances or business associates of Joe Cannelli. There seems to be some sort of tie-in."

"As a matter of fact, Morley, I am an acquaintance of Joe Cannelli. A lot of people know him. He's supposed to be a gambler."

"Well," sighed Francis, "I suspect that he's gambling with lives right now, though I don't wish to sound like Pegler."

"By the way," asked Starr, "did the Tiger get hold of that Holden diary?"

"Why no—" Francis was interrupted by the buzzing of the intercom. He answered this to hear Hattie ask:

"Is Captain Starr there? I have a very urgent call for him."

"Oh, well put them on."

Francis handed the phone to Starr, who answered gruffly, and then listened with an excited interest. He hung up and got to his feet. Standing over Francis, he asked, "You're sure that you can back all this up, everything you've told me here?"

"Captain, I have said there were witnesses."

"Okay, okay. Now we've got another angle. They've kidnapped Vivien Holden."

"They've what?"

"Yeah. A couple of guys got to her apartment a little after seven this morning, tied her up and started searching. Then the maid came in, and they tied her up, too. They hunted everywhere, nearly wrecked the place. Then they took the Holden girl away."

"What in the world were they looking for?"

"A book of some kind. I've a feeling it might have been the diary."

"But, Captain, nobody knew about that. She only remembered it as she was leaving here late yesterday afternoon. I told you last night, and also Tiger heard her. But when he took her home, I guess they both forgot all about it. At least that's what he said this morning. So who else knew about it?"

The police officer shook his head.

"It beats me! Didn't Olsen say anything about it at all?"

"Uh-uh, except that he had forgotten about it. Say, what time did you say—at seven this morning?"

Captain Starr nodded.

Francis considered for a minute, then said, "Well, I personally think that this all ties in with the Baths. Now, if we can believe that, then we can believe that Buster may have been the one that blackmailed and killed the Holden girl's brother. Now there comes up a mention of his having kept a diary. At seven in the morning kidnappers call on Vivien, the murdered man's sister, who might have the diary. Okay—" Francis paused as he saw where this cumulative reasoning was taking him.

Captain Starr said impatiently, "Yeah—?"

"Well," continued Francis, "to my own personal knowledge, Buster was suddenly called away from a very profitable job of photography just before seven this morning. And, a half hour later, the manager of the Baths was clearing everyone out of the upper floors there. I'll bet—"

The detective officer snatched at the phone, but Francis stayed his arm. He looked unsmilingly into the officer's eyes.

"Yes, I think so too. But you'll have a rough time getting in. I honestly believe that all they'll want from the girl is the diary, if there is one. Possibly some ransom money. I mean, I don't think that she's in any immediate danger. Now, I ask you to give me two hours. Tiger and I can easily get back in there; and we know the layout. And, Captain, after all, she's my client."

The policeman's hand relaxed on the telephone as he considered this. Finally he nodded. "Okay, it's eleven now. At one o'clock, we'll come into that joint—and strong! Meantime, do what you can."

As the officer turned to leave, Francis said, "Why don't you run down those property owners, Captain. And, oh, by the way, I just remembered something. Someone, somewhere last night, said something about someone named Bruce. If there is such a person, he might be the big one."

Captain Starr stopped as if pole-axed. Without even turning around, he asked, "You're sure the name was Bruce?"

"Sure, I'm sure! Some old character at the Baths made some crack about Bruce raising the prices. Why?"

"Bruce! Christ! I should have known better. The diary—"

"Say, Captain Starr, what's the matter?"

Francis reached into a desk drawer and took out a glass, with the bottle of pungent Greek brandy. He quickly poured a large measure and handed it to the homicide officer.

Starr, still standing like a man in shock, took the drink and downed it. He shuddered, and then, carefully setting the empty glass on the desk, turned again to the door. Here he paused, hand on the knob.

"Well, we'd better find her. I know now how they found out about the diary. I told them."

With this cryptic remark, the police captain strode from the room, slamming the door behind him.

Chapter Seventeen

Francis parked the car hastily in an opening at the curb. The neighborhood was busier now at midday, though it was still an obvious backwash of the busy city. He had quickly briefed Tiger on his concept of the situation, and between them they had come to an identical conclusion.

If this was where Vivien was being held—and both thought that it probably was—they were fairly sure that she would be on the more private upper floors. Also, they realized that they had little more than an hour; and it would take some time for them to get into the place in a natural way. This possibly halved their time in which to find the girl before the police arrived and broke it all up.

"Why don't we just let 'em do it?" asked Tiger.

Francis shook his head stubbornly.

"No, I've been thinking about this, and while it may seem like a pretty mercenary point of view, it's the way I feel about it. Y'see, Tiger, we've gotten mixed up in something pretty nasty here. If we help the police to break it all up, that's okay. But we, the Agency, have spent a lot of time and money getting this far. Now, as I see it, we've got a client, a customer—Vivien Holden. She hired us to find her brother. Well, we found him. As a matter of fact, we knew where he was, but he was dead. Now our investigation has got our client kidnapped. Okay, maybe we can get her out of there if she's still safe and sound. In this case, and if we are right, we will have solved his murder at least. In any case, the police are going to get all the credit for it. But I think with this much accomplished we can send the young lady a bill without feeling too badly about it. After all, she's got the money. Well, what do you think, Olsen?"

Tiger hesitated, shaking his head grimly. "Hell! I don't know, Frank. I guess you're right. Well, hell, let's find her first."

Francis gave his assistant a long look, and then smiled easily. "Crazy, man! Come on, you big mass of muscles, let's do it!"

With this they left the car and crossed the street to the Baths, where as they entered Tiger murmured, "Here we go again, boys..."

It was Francis' hope that the attendants who had seen them the night before would now have been replaced by a day shift, and in this they were lucky. Quickly registering, then, they told the blondined character at the desk that they wouldn't be in for long, and so wouldn't bother to check anything. This brought a knowing leer from the extrovert under the tied-and-dyed hair and a "gay" remark suggesting procedure. The two hurried on into the long, cubicle-filled room.

The stairs to the upper floors were to the left. Kate had been relieved by another attendant who sprawled in a chair placed across the bottom step. The Agency men proceeded with their hastily devised plan. Fortunately, their assigned "rooms" were toward the rear; but on this same side there seemed to be only one or two bathers strolling about.

Francis and Tiger quickly entered one of the little rooms, and at once started a scuffling noise, which rapidly grew in volume. From without it could easily have sounded like a serious altercation or a fight. The plan worked like a charm, quickly bringing the attendant, who knocked forcefully on the door.

"Hey! What's going on in there? Can't you guys do it quietly?"

Francis moaned convincingly. Tiger, partly concealed behind the door, fumbled open the latch. Then, from the rear of the little room, Francis moaned again, adding dramatically, "Oh, please come in and help me."

The attendant pushed the door open, and seeing only Francis cowering in the far corner with his arms about his head, he came on into the cubicle, asking very rudely, "What the hell's the matter with you, dearie?"

This was his last remark for some time; the Tiger gave him a simple judo cut behind the ear that dropped him unconscious at their feet. Francis quickly relieved him of the large bunch of keys that hung from his belt, and the limp attendant was shoved back under the narrow bed. Olsen gazed wonderingly at his open hand.

"Hey, Frank, I always wanted to see if that would work."

"Silly boy! Come on, I've got the keys. We'll just walk quietly. Leave this one here. He'll keep."

They met no one on their way to the stairs, nor on the way up to the next floor. Here Francis whispered to Tiger, "I'll go on up to the third while you look through these rooms down here." At Olsen's nodded agreement, Francis continued on up the stairs.

Tiger turned to the nearest door, which led into one of the "viewing" rooms, though he hardly recalled the exact layout here. He only vaguely remembered the briefing he had had earlier in the morning.

The room he entered was dark, but Tiger could clearly hear sighs and moans, gasps for breath, and the faint creaking of a bed in use, all of which could only indicate that at least two people were struggling furiously in the dark. As he stood motionless listening, a sudden lift of one hand caused it to brush across a curtain of some sort. Tiger heard a faint tingle, like that of a ring on metal. The vibrant and passionate breathings of two people continued without interruption.

Somehow these faintly guttural noises reminded him of something, or someone, but just what escaped him at the moment. Almost at once he realized that the unseen pair were not exactly fighting.

Suddenly, Tiger remembered the two-way windows. He tried to recall whether they were curtained on both sides. Yeah! That old guy had said you could hear it all from next door as well as watch!

Carefully, Tiger ran his hands over the hanging material. Yes! These were short drapes that covered a glass pane. Finding their center, he cautiously drew them apart... and stood completely dumfounded by the picture that met his eyes.

One of the two sweaty bodies writhing in a posture of sex was clearly and dearly familiar to Tiger. The instant thought of rescue was quickly abandoned when he realized that here was no rape, no forceful taking of the woman who had been so quiescently pliant beneath him only a few hours before.

This was a maddened, abandoned, wild creature— moaning, clasping, biting; straining at the body that violently twisted and contorted itself with her own. Sweat broke out on Olsen's brow as, for a single instant, the two beyond the window seemed to pause at the very pinnacle of violence and motion.

Vivien's lithe and perfect body, glisteningly drenched with perspiration, lay momentarily stretched out. Her head and shoulders were bent almost double—like an animate figure "six." In its classic and momentary immobility her body might have been likened to a classic Grecian sculpture.

Complementing this and equally as artistically attractive was the bronzed powerful body of the man. His lower limbs were almost outstretched and his upper body was inversely twisted into a complementing duplicate of her pose. Fleetingly, the pair could have brought to mind an advertising poster that might use classic figures bent in shapes of numerals. He lay a panting "nine" above, beside, and around her, encompassing for the fleeting moment her gracious "six."

As the two so paused in their frenzied play—as if to draw the last possible bit of passion and response from each other—Tiger's eyes noted the clothing, torn and flung to one side. He saw, too, a short-handled whip with knotted thongs of leather. Hurled down as if useless, were several small rattan canes. These and other objects that appeared to have been employed but briefly and discarded strewed the floor about the great bed.

Tiger's questing eyes and alerted mind took all this in in a matter of seconds. His own features simultaneously blushed at the thoughts and memories his mind sent racing through his massive body. Even as he stared, the great muscled lover's body fell away from Vivien as though tired and deflated. His strong hands fumbled in her tousled hair, pulling her eager head away from his tired flesh.

The acoustics were so excellent that Tiger could hear a faint mouth sound as her lips were pulled steadily away from the man's reddened and spent body. Even as he pulled her around so that she lay half across him, the man reached roughly for one pendant breast, across which blood-streaked lines showed. Almost as a man admitting defeat, the tired eyes beneath the beetling brows met the girl's triumphant ones. She laughed dryly, then more shrilly, then joyously and victoriously.

In a moment, the man reached down, his huge biceps indicating his great power and strength as he pulled the girl's body up to and onto his own. For a moment he held her suspended above him, and then impulsively clasped her to him. Just the single note of another peal of mad laughter escaped her mouth before he caught and buried it and her lips between his own. Fiercely, roughly, he hugged her to him. To the unseen and unsensed observer, it seemed as if the man's passion would break her in two. Then, in another swift movement, he again held her away from himself and pantingly demanded, "Damn you! Where's the diary?"

Lightly, as if in the middle of an innocent social conversation, she jibed, "And you thought that you could hurt me! You've beaten me, whipped me, taken me roughly and painfully, and I've gone you better every time. It's you who are tired of it now, you who wants to stop."

She laughed again, this time with a note of scorn apparent in her voice, scorn clear even to Olsen who could hardly believe that this wanton was the girl he had forcefully, manfully, but tenderly and naturally seduced a few hours before.

Could this be the girl who had been for a time afraid of being hurt, who had whimpered softly with pain as he had lain upon her?

Olsen shook his head to get the cobwebs of memory from it. As he watched, enthralled and almost unbelieving, Vivien pulled roughly away from the man beneath her and flung herself to one side of the great bed. One of her dainty hands reached out tentatively. With a disdainful fingertip, she flicked the man's limp penis.

"You can't hurt me, Buster, as big as you are." She laughed wildly.

For a moment the man lay inert beside her, then he jumped to his feet. He grabbed up a robe from the floor and shrugged into it. Walking around the bed, he stood beside and over her. Even as he stood there, breathing deeply, his shaking shoulders indicated to Tiger his great anger and frustration. Vivien gazed up at him, smiling. She languidly raised her hands to part his robe.

With one huge hand he knocked hers aside; with the other he grabbed her by the hair. His rage was now obvious to the girl, and his efforts to contain his madness caused his entire body to shiver.

Pulling her up from the bed by her hair, he said, "I'll hurt you, you greedy bitch! I'll hurt you! I'll kill you! But before I do that I'll tell you something that will take the grin off that greedy hot mouth of yours. Yes, I'll tell you something that will really hurt you, and then I'll kill you! You won't be the first I've killed. Do you know who the first was? Yeah! Now I interest you, don't I? Well, I beat him, too, and whipped him, and did everything to him that I've done to you! And he liked it. He begged for more, and he paid money, too."

The hulking, hovering man, insane with his rage, shook the woman as if she were a rag doll. His voice was now a shout of triumph as he went on, "Yes, I said 'he.' Oh, he loved it, too! It must run in your rotten family. Sure, that's right. You're as perverted as he was! And so you want to be beaten some more, and whipped and used, do you? But I can't hurt you, you think! Well, I can kill you—just like I killed your precious brother."

A little scream came from Vivien, and for the first time in these seemingly endless minutes that had passed so timelessly before him, Tiger saw pain and fright and returning normalcy in the girl's eyes. She tried desperately to pull away as Buster grabbed her by the throat. Even as the big hands clasped themselves around her neck, and Tiger started to turn towards the door he had blundered through only a few minutes before, an alarm bell sounded through the hall loud and insistently.

Tiger's eyes turned back to the window in time to see a desperate Buster drop the girl and leap to the door of the party room. There he paused but a second. Tiger knew that he must have pressed some hidden button, because the door promptly swung wide. Buster ran quickly through, slamming it behind him.

As he watched, spellbound with all he had seen, Tiger saw the girl—again appearing to be the sweet, frail creature he had met only yesterday afternoon—fall back crying on the great bed in which she had pleasured herself so completely and unreservedly and unnaturally just a few minutes before. Her little tongue darted out of her open mouth and ran seeking around her lips. She smiled, as though savoring again the taste of something delicious.

Chapter Eighteen

On the floor above, Francis faced a long hallway with several closed doors on either side. A few ceiling lights burned dimly, and at the far end a window was unshaded but crudely painted over. Bright spears of light filtered through this rude blackout in spots where the paint had peeled away. On closer examination Francis saw that this window was also nailed shut; a glimpse through one of the scaling paint holes, showed only emptiness which reached down and farther down to the faintly heard noises of the traffic on the freeway far below.

Turning to the door on one hand, Francis tried the knob and was not surprised to find it locked. The third key opened the door, admitting him to an ordinary if slightly dusty and meanly furnished office.

A small safe stood in one corner with its door ajar. A partly opened door revealed a closet that was bare except for some photographic supplies on the shelves. Another door was closed on a bare and utilitarian bathroom, whose principal piece of furniture was a bucket-like old iron bathtub propped up agedly on unbelievable claw feet. A moth-eaten sofa cowered against one wall of the office, and long heavy drapes concealed most of another. Drawn back, these disclosed a large window that looked out pleasantly over the sunlit city.

Francis spent little time with this handsome view, but quickly turned to the desk in the center of the room. Its top was littered with odd papers and a few photographs. These were at once apparent as products of the house photographer, and were certainly not meant for public viewing.

With a grunt of disgust, the Agency man tore these across and dropped them into a large metal utility wastebasket. With the glimmerings of an idea, he quickly added the hastily inspected letters and other papers from the desktop. One unlocked drawer yielded a bunch of small photos showing more natural activities and a small packet of booklets of the "Tillie and Mac" type. Assuming that these last might just be casually amusing on some future dull occasion, if not immediately pertinent to the matter at hand, Francis slipped the booklets into his pocket. The other drawers of the desk, which he quickly pried open, seemed to hold nothing of importance. All papers that he found were added to the mass in the basket. A bottle and some glasses were left as they were. Some small packets of folded paper that contained a white crystalline powder, he also left intact.

Crossing to the safe, Francis edged the heavy door open, and first found a small but businesslike file inside. Several reference books of the *Who's-Who* type, a city directory, and some simple lists of names and addresses bound into pamphlets were also among the safe's contents. The pamphlets Francis assumed to be the usual professional sucker lists, and he thought that they also might be of some future use. Pocketing these, he next found, to his considerable surprise, a heavy manila envelope containing a thick sheaf of currency. A quick glance showed a predominance of hundred dollar bills. Holding this in his hands for the briefest of moments, Francis considered that he was as honest as the next man and stuffed it away carefully in an inside pocket.

The letter file proved to be of even more interest. In alphabetical order were photos, letters, registration cards for the Baths below, and in most cases small ledger sheets showing notations of various sums of money and appended with cryptic and undecipherable notes. Each grouping seemed to cover fully a period of visits to the Baths, then to the "party" rooms, with detailed photos covering these later visits. The ledger notations undoubtedly listed the further tribute occasioned by these pictured visits.

There were over fifty individual files. The photographs brought blushes even to Francis. He impulsively dumped the whole file and its contents into the well-filled waste container.

Francis began to realize that he had spent some time in this one room and that there might be little enough time left to find the girl, but he could not resist the impulse that made him pause, set his gun down on the corner of the desk, gather up the loaded waste basket and carry it into the bathroom. Here he dumped everything into the huge iron tub and, with a flick of his lighter, set them afire.

With a smile on his face, he stepped back into the office, closing the bathroom door behind him, just as the hall door burst open. A huge, disheveled and angry man rushed into the room, holding a dressing gown about his massively muscular torso.

Both men stopped for an instant. Then Francis, intent on edging toward the gun he had carelessly left on the desk, involuntarily glanced in that direction. This alerted the robed intruder, who bellowed, "Who the hell are you?"—and without waiting at all for an answer, also leapt toward the weapon.

In his rush, Buster's head and shoulders were well protruded. Francis paused, seeing that he couldn't reach the gun first, and neatly but heavily drop-kicked the heavy chin. Buster's head snapped back and he stumbled, falling across one corner of the desk. The force of his fall knocked the gun to the floor, where it slid under the sofa.

As if in answer to the question put him, Francis, now edging toward the door, replied, "I'm Morley. And you must be Buster."

The big man in the robe rose from the desk, shook his head and felt his jaw gingerly. Then, noting Francis' intention, he stalked across the room. As soon as he was near enough he launched a devastating blow at the calmer Agency man. Francis ducked this neatly and sidestepped, as he cooly demanded, "Where's the girl?"

Again trying to slug Francis, the burly photographer swore awesomely, but did reply, "That goddamned nympho! She's downstairs, and as soon as I get you, I'll take care of her…"

Francis again avoided a rush, though not completely. The edge of the heavily swung fist caught him alongside his ear. Even though Morley did not get the full power of the blow—his attacker was obviously both hurt and winded—it rocked him back and made him acutely aware of his immediate danger. The bull-like Buster set himself for another swing.

Francis coolly coordinated his own slighter body, allowing the sledge-like blow to pass close by his head. However, instead of backing away, he moved in swiftly and grasped the folds of his opponent's robe. With a secure grasp of the heavy fabric and a guiding elbow to the bigger man's hip, Francis dropped backwards to the floor, neatly kicking Buster's feet out from under him.

The fall and the big man's off-balance weight pivoted nicely against Francis' stiff arm in this elemental judo throw. The Agency man was pleased to see and feel his bulkier adversary helplessly and with swift momentum swing up and over him.

Expecting to hear the released body land in a corner with a crushingly satisfactory thud, Francis was shocked at the noisy crash of breaking glass.

After a long, single second, he heard the fast receding scream of a man falling through space.

Turning on one knee, Francis saw that he was alone in the room. A draft of cool summer air came in through the shattered remnants of the big window.

Shaking his head to clear it from the single blow he had received, Francis retrieved his gun and, pausing only to make sure the fire in the bathroom was burning nicely, fled from the office. In the hallway he heard shouts from below. The place had become a bedlam of noises.

Racing down the stairs, he met Tiger, who was half consoling, half supporting a very disheveled Vivien. She was draped and partially wrapped in an oversized bedspread, and for all the urgency and seriousness of the occasion, Francis had the rather alien thought that she looked rather cute, if not downright desirable. The bedspread, as large as it was, was doing little to cover certain important portions of her body. But this was no time to ponder the lovely mysteries of Vivien Holden.

The sound of a force of men breaking into the building on the floor below spurred Francis into a split decision. He indicated the stairs that led to the side door and shooed Tiger and Vivien quickly down them.

The three were across the street, into the car and away just before the block became completely entangled with arriving police cars, ambulances and fire equipment.

Driving quickly away from the building that now belched smoke and flames from the roof and one side, Francis' smile was more or less smug as he patted his full pockets. It was even smugger when from the corner of his eye he saw Tiger the Rescuer patting something else equally as full. On they sped, Francis never slowing as he careened around a hard left turn.

Chapter Nineteen

It was the next day, nearly noon. Tiger and Francis had again compared notes, after a more or less complete going over of the whole business with the police and a man from the District Attorney's office the evening before. They had finally dictated to Hattie a discreet report of what Francis would always feel could only be the Agency's maddest case.

After reminding their girl-of-all-work of the utmost secrecy of the data given her and astounding her with a very generous check in four figures—which was Vivien Holden's contribution just prior to her sudden departure on an extended world cruise—Francis leaned back in the chair behind his desk.

"Well, muscles, now that you've rested, what do you think of our little Agency?"

"Huh! Get her," Tiger grinned.

Francis interrupted, with a hint of annoyance in his eye. "Just for the record, Mr. Olsen, let me do the camping in this act. I'll make with the gay talk. You just be big and beasty. Okay?"

The big, handsome ex-Marine sensed that his employer was not altogether joking, but he only had the opportunity to shrug an acknowledgment of this when the door opened and Captain Starr walked in.

Francis greeted him cordially: "Hello, Captain. Say, don't you ever knock? Why, for all you know, Tiger and I might have been in an, er, embarrassing position."

"Knock it off, Morley," said the big detective officer, with a nodded greeting for Tiger as well. "I thought that we'd have one more little talk. And if there are any angles that we didn't get around to with the D.A. last evening, we could clear it up now."

The official flung a late paper on Francis' desk and slumped into a convenient chair and crossed his legs comfortably. Tiger noticed the small bandage on the palm of the Captain's hand and casually remarked, "What happened to your hand, John? Cut y'self?"

The Captain flushed, but after a second he replied evenly and almost as casually, "Nope, got bit by a dog. Trying to give this pup some worm medicine, y'see, and he nipped my hand."

During this brief exchange, Francis had been scanning the headlines which read, "CITY MOURNS SENATOR MARTIN." The lengthy and laudatory story that followed gave the highlights of Martin's career as a public official and leading citizen. Reading with only partial interest, Francis noted that the body had been found by Captain of Detectives John Starr, a close personal friend who had called socially on the Senator late on the preceding afternoon.

Raising his eyes from the newspaper, Francis met those of the police officer.

"Oh, Captain, so that's where you were late yesterday afternoon. 'Close personal friend'... well. I'm sorry, sir. Believe me."

"Did you know that Tiger knew him, too?" asked the Captain.

"We weren't really well acquainted, John," Tiger spoke up. "I used to see him around, but mostly at the Back Room."

"Well, gentlemen," said Francis, "you both have my sincere condolences. Tough, Captain, that you should walk in on his body."

Captain Starr nodded.

"Yes, I went to see Bruce—Bruce Martin, that is, or was—about a personal matter. Nothing important now. His houseboy was there, but he hadn't bothered to call the Senator, who kept pretty late hours and liked to sleep in the daytime. Well, I guess he wasn't well; pretty old, too. But, anyway, he had this bunch of medicines in bottles on a table alongside his bed. Mostly plain ordinary stuff like aspirin and sleeping pills. But there was one bottle that was labeled 'poison.' This was some kind of potent heart stimulant. His doctor says that he was subject to mild attacks and that those pills were strictly for an emergency and never to be taken more than one at a time. It appears that he must have reached for the aspirins and somehow got the wrong bottle, taking three or four of the 'poison' tablets. At least, that's what the doctors all agree."

Francis had become very quiet during this almost unnecessary recital, and after a pause following Starr's last words, he remarked casually, "Definitely accidental, then?"

For a long moment, Starr's eyes met Morley's. There seemed to be present in the room a note of hovering tension, which was snapped abruptly as Tiger remarked, "Francis, this is the police. He oughta know! Heck, you don't suppose that someone held the man's mouth and forced the

133

pills down him—and then held him while he swallowed and passed out, do you?"

Francis gazed steadily at the neat bandage on the police captain's upturned palm. Again his eyes met Starr's. After a long minute, Francis lowered his glance and reached for a cigarette. Lighting it, he mused, just audibly, "Bruce Martin... Bruce..."

Snapping his lighter shut decisively, he brightened and turned to his assistant.

"Well, Tiger," he said quite cheerily, "I suppose you'll want to go to the funeral. Okay. Now, Captain Starr, let's pick up all of our loose ends. Just where does the case stand now?"

"Say, John," interrupted Tiger, "Frank and I sort of feel that there is some number one man, a big shot, in this somewhere—"

"No, Tiger!" Francis cut in sharply. "I think that we were wrong there. I feel now that Buster masterminded the whole deal, except for the narcotics; and that was Cannelli's tie-in. What do you think, Captain Starr? Or has Cannelli given you anyone else?"

"No. Joe is pleading guilty to a narcotics charge. They're federal anyway. But he will not implicate anyone else. That's definite. I, er, had a talk with him."

"Well, if you think so. Possibly there's no one else to be implicated, like Frank says; but still, I sort of thought for awhile there..." remarked Olsen.

Captain Starr rose from his chair. "I guess this washes up our three murders, then. It's very handy that the tape recorder was on in that party room where Buster had the girl, and that Tiger brought the tape out with him as well as the girl. This pretty much ties it all up with Buster, and the department is closing the cases on that note."

Tiger laughed shortly. "It was even luckier that we got ourselves out of there before the building went down! Have you seen it since, John?"

"Yes, I drove out by there this morning. The whole place was pretty old, and the wood was dry. It went pretty fast."

"I suppose so. Lucky that no one except Buster got hurt."

"Yes," said Starr. "The police now feel that he must have been trapped up there in his office, and either fell or deliberately jumped from that window. The fire department thinks that the fire started in some loose photographic equipment, chemicals or something. It's hard to tell, there's so little left of the building. Yes, I guess that about washes it all up, Morley. I, er, suppose that the department owes the Agency some considerable thanks. Er, unofficially, of course. And you know that you have mine—for everything. You men managed a good police job on this. And—well, thanks!"

Tiger grinned. "I told you, John."

Starr flushed, then added, "I'll admit, Morley, if Olsen hadn't convinced me that you were okay, we wouldn't even have got started on this. I had some ideas. Well, I admit that I was probably wrong."

Francis, now also standing, put one hand on his hip and smoothed his wavy hair with the other in an unmistakable gesture as he gushed, "Oh, Captain Starr! I bet you tell that to all the boys..."

The police officer strode to the door, shaking his head. There he turned and glared at Tiger.

"I just don't get it..."

The officer, hand on the door, was about to leave when, in a more serious tone, Francis stopped him. He paused, turning his head.

"Captain, you'd better take it easy in the future when giving medicine to sick dogs. You might get more seriously bitten."

The detective's eyes dropped to his bandaged hand. Then he looked at Francis. Turning so as to include Tiger, and with a slight smile, he said, "See you men around." He went out, closing the door gently behind him.

During this last, Tiger had picked up the discarded newspaper. After a wave of the hand at the departing Starr, he remarked, "I always read this guy Kane. Say, have you seen his column yet, Frank?"

"Nope! Been too busy. Think I'll have a workout at the gym this afternoon. What about you?"

Tiger had been reading the paper and now looked up angrily.

"Say, I don't think I like this."

"What?"

"Oh, it's Bert. Bert Kane. He's kidding people all the time. But this is kinda snotty..."

He passed the paper back to Francis, who quickly found Kane's column. About in the middle of it, he found:

Friday Frittata: "that old gang of mine." Only last Monday we all gathered around the big table in Flanagan's Back Room. Senator Bruce Martin, Captain John Starr (of the police stars—get it?), Joe Cannelli, the restaurateur, Tiger Olsen, the ex-Marine and late car salesman, and myself! We all laughed merrily at some mention of the gay set, including one of Joe's employees, and also about a new member of our swish set who has inherited a local detective agency. Joy was unrefined! Today, the papers headline the tragic death of kindly Senator Martin, long the City's leading citizen. He was found, shortly after death, by his old friend Captain Starr, who, peculiarly, had gone to tell him of the astounding arrest of Joe Cannelli as a drug dealer. Also noted: the ex-Marine, ex-MAN-about-town Tiger Olsen, has gone to work for the exchorus boy who is now a detective! And, worse and worse, girls, though there seems to be no connection, the Baths have burned down! Whatta week!

Francis read through this and laughed wholeheartedly, but Tiger was still annoyed.

"Hell, Frank! Bert and I have been pretty good friends, and this is kinda nasty."

"Well, dearie, you've got broad shoulders. Don't let it worry you. It's all in fun. Just the same, that one better never let me catch her with her hair down..." Tiger shook his head: "Uh-uh, Frank. I don't think he's—"

"Huh!" snorted Francis. "I always say that anyone knowing that much of the words and music is bound to have done the dance routines too! By the way, I forgot..." Francis pulled some money from a pocket and laid several large bills on the desk. "And, another thing I'm always saying is something about not looking at either end of gift horses. Anyway, we got a sort of cash bonus on this deal. If your conscience doesn't bother you any more than mine, you'll pick up your share."

Hesitantly, Olsen drew the money towards himself, then picked it up and pocketed it, with a slightly questioning look at his employer.

"Just let's say that I found it in the fire. If I hadn't picked it up, it would have gone up in smoke. And I don't think that any living soul has a claim on it. Satisfy you?"

After a moment, Tiger matched Francis' smile with one of his own.

"Whatta job! And whatta boss! Eh, boss?"

At this moment, a disturbance in the outer office was clearly evident. Both men turned that way as the door flew open and in stalked a very agitated and slightly disheveled elderly lady bearing a traveling pet cage. This she set down roughly on Francis' desk. Then, fixing him with a beady eye, she declared, "You, sir, are a charlatan!"

"Ah, yes, and a bright good morning—or is it now after-noon?—to you, too, Mrs. Bagnold."

"This beast that you foisted off on me is not the Emir of Afghanistan." Turning on Tiger, she included him in her wrath. "And you, sir! You should be ashamed! Introducing this—this fiend into my innocent household."

"Well, madam," pleaded Olsen, "I was almost positively sure from your description that this was your pet. Are you very sure? That is—"

"Yes, Mrs. Bagnold," offered Francis. "You did say they all looked somewhat alike. Perhaps he's just upset, being away from his home and all those—"

"Mr. Morley! Let's have no more of this gross deception. This is not the animal my sister sent to me—the Emir. And I am quite sure of it! Her reason for sending the Emir was that she thought he should have a change of surroundings after his operation. For two days and nights now, this beast and my three poor innocent Persians have made my home a shambles—until we were finally able to catch this monster! Believe me, gentlemen, this is not the Emir. He has very definitely never been operated on."

Tiger hid his face in his handkerchief with a burst of spurious coughing. Francis just managed to restrain his mirth as he replied with dignity, "Madame, if there has been an error, my secretary will give you a check in full refund of your fee."

For a moment, the austere dowager allowed a look of kindly reminiscence to show on her face.

"That won't be necessary, young man. The, er, display was, er, interesting! However, should my darlings, er, conceive as a result of this unprincipled feline's aggressiveness, I shall seriously consider naming you in a paternity suit."

With this she stalked to the door, where she paused. Turning back, she added with a sigh, "Truly, it was magnificent. Believe me! All three in one afternoon! I just want to be sure that you will take good care of this over-energetic beast. I do realize that it was all a mistake. But, well, at my age, it's just too much! Good day, gentlemen—and you, too, you thing!"

With this Mrs. Bagnold flounced out. Hattie came in to find Francis and Tiger limp with laughter.

The cat in the cage paused in washing its wise face to eye this new female.

"Well, Mr. Morley, and what do we do with it?" demanded Hattie.

Catching his breath, Francis roared, "Get her! Call him Butch and put him on the payroll. After all, we need some live pussy around this office."

The cat said, "Mmrrroww!"